# AMBUSHED!

Longarm shook the match out and tossed it away.

Just then, a sheet of flame blossomed in the mouth of an alley across the street.

The bright, yellow-gold flower of fire had a long spike in the center of it. And that fiery, lead-tipped spear was pointed square at Longarm. The sight of the flame was accompanied by the roar of a gunshot half a heartbeat later.

Too late to do any good but unable to resist the impulse, Longarm ducked.

By that time, the slug from the ambusher's gun had already buried itself in the boards that sheathed the false front of the saloon Longarm had just left.

He triggered three fast, searching rounds into the shadowy mouth of the alley, then spun and darted back the way he'd just come.

It would've been heroic as hell to charge straight across into that alley with his gun blazing and a gleam in his eye.

It also would have been dumb as hell.

\*    \*    \*

***SPECIAL PREVIEW!***

**Turn to the back of this book for a sneak-peek excerpt from the exciting, brand new Western series . . .**

**FURY**

**. . . the blazing story of a gunfighting legend.**

*Also in the LONGARM series*
*from Jove*

LONGARM

LONGARM AND THE
LONE STAR LEGEND

LONGARM AND THE
LONE STAR BOUNTY

LONGARM AND THE
LONE STAR RUSTLERS

LONGARM AND THE
LONE STAR DELIVERANCE

LONGARM IN THE
TEXAS PANHANDLE

LONGARM AND THE
RANCHER'S SHOWDOWN

LONGARM ON THE
INLAND PASSAGE

LONGARM IN THE
RUBY RANGE COUNTRY

LONGARM AND THE
GREAT CATTLE KILL

LONGARM AND THE
CROOKED RAILMAN

LONGARM ON THE SIWASH TRAIL

LONGARM AND THE
RUNAWAY THIEVES

LONGARM AND THE
ESCAPE ARTIST

LONGARM IN THE BIG BURNOUT

LONGARM AND THE
TREACHEROUS TRIAL

LONGARM AND THE
NEW MEXICO SHOOT-OUT

LONGARM AND THE
LONE STAR FRAME

LONGARM AND THE
RENEGADE SERGEANT

LONGARM IN THE SIERRA MADRES

LONGARM AND THE
HANGMAN'S LIST

LONGARM IN THE CLEARWATERS

LONGARM AND THE
REDWOOD RAIDERS

LONGARM AND THE
DEADLY JAILBREAK

LONGARM AND THE PAWNEE KID

LONGARM AND THE
DEVIL'S STAGECOACH

LONGARM AND THE
WYOMING BLOODBATH

LONGARM IN THE RED DESERT

LONGARM AND THE
CROOKED MARSHAL

LONGARM AND THE
TEXAS RANGERS

LONGARM AND THE VIGILANTES

LONGARM IN THE OSAGE STRIP

LONGARM AND THE LOST MINE

LONGARM AND THE
LONGLEY LEGEND

LONGARM AND THE
DEAD MAN'S BADGE

LONGARM AND THE
KILLER'S SHADOW

LONGARM AND THE
MONTANA MASSACRE

LONGARM IN THE
MEXICAN BADLANDS

LONGARM AND THE
BOUNTY HUNTRESS

LONGARM AND THE
DENVER BUST-OUT

LONGARM AND THE SKULL
CANYON GANG

LONGARM AND THE
RAILROAD TO HELL

LONGARM AND THE
LONE STAR CAPTIVE

LONGARM AND THE
GOLD HUNTERS

LONGARM AND THE
COLORADO GUNDOWN

LONGARM AND THE
GRAVE ROBBERS

LONGARM AND THE
ARKANSAS AMBUSH

LONGARM AND THE
ARIZONA SHOWDOWN

LONGARM AND THE
UTE NATION

LONGARM IN THE
SIERRA ORIENTAL

LONGARM AND THE
GUNSLICKS

LONGARM AND THE
LADY SHERIFF

LONGARM ON THE
DEVIL'S HIGHWAY

→ TABOR EVANS →

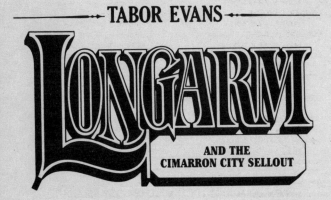

# LONGARM

### AND THE
### CIMARRON CITY SELLOUT

JOVE BOOKS, NEW YORK

LONGARM AND THE CIMARRON CITY SELLOUT

A Jove Book / published by arrangement with
the author

PRINTING HISTORY
Jove edition / July 1992

ISBN: 0-515-10880-4

Jove Books are published by The Berkley Publishing Group,
200 Madison Avenue, New York, New York 10016.
The name "JOVE" and the "J" logo
are trademarks belonging to Jove Publications, Inc.

PRINTED IN THE UNITED STATES OF AMERICA

10  9  8  7  6  5  4  3  2  1

# Chapter 1

The tall, broad-shouldered man slipped cautiously through the door and stepped immediately to the side, remaining under the shaded overhang where it would not be so easy for anyone on the street to spot him. He fidgeted nervously with his watch chain as he stood, as alert and cautious as a stag listening to hounds, with his back pressed against the glass. His eyes cut rapidly left and right and left again. A hack rolled past, its driver paying no attention to the people on the street nearby. The tall man watched it with suspicion and only relaxed when the cab was out of sight again. Any vehicle, any doorway, any window might conceal the pursuer.

The hack turned a corner and was gone. A heavy dray rumbled into view and out again without pausing. Passersby strode by on the sidewalk without a glance. So far so good. So far all seemed safe enough.

The tall man swallowed, looked once more to both sides and then committed himself to public view. He stepped away from the café where he'd taken his breakfast—a restaurant he had never patronized before as it would not have been wise to appear at any of his usual favorites—and moved quickly toward the maze of alleys and side streets that would allow him to approach the stone facade of the Federal Building without being detected.

Or so he hoped.

The problem, dammit, was that he had to reach that destination. For all practical purposes he had no choice about it. And anyone who knew him at all well would know it. He was limited. The other was not. It is always the hunter, never the quarry, who has the choice of the stalking ground. Dammit.

He walked quickly, almost at a trot, his long legs speeding him along at a pace few might match without breaking into a run.

He was more than six feet in height and lean despite the width and power of his shoulders. His hips were narrow and his belly flat. He was deemed handsome by others, though he thought of himself as being more craggy and "interesting." His hair was brown, matching a thick sweep of dark brown mustache. His face was tanned and weathered, his eyes a luminous and sometimes golden brown.

He wore a tweed coat, corduroy trousers, and a snuff brown, flat-crowned Stetson hat. His stovepipe cavalryman's boots were black leather. So was a gunbelt that rode prominently at his waist. The holster there was positioned on his belly just to the left of his belt buckle and was canted for a right-handed crossdraw . . . or quite as easily for an only slightly awkward left hand draw if need should arise.

He gave the impression of a man who was confident of his strengths.

But not at this particular moment.

Right now he seemed more apprehensive than strong.

He licked dry lips and moved quickly along a carefully planned route of approach, peering nervously in one direction and then another as he sought to avoid the confrontation that was threatened. If he could only spot the ambush in time, turn aside in time, slip away, and thus escape the face to face encounter. . . .

Slim chance is better than none. Even if the other did know his destination there was at least that chance that he might yet avoid detection.

He darted into the protection of an alley, dashed quickly across the next street over, and passed through the gates of the Denver Mint—that should fox the pursuit, dammit; no one without federal authorization could follow in there—and traversed that entire city block without having to show himself on the public streets.

Only seventy five yards or so to go now, and so far so good. He paused to catch his breath and gather himself for the last rush. There was no way to avoid it. Here he had to be in plain view of anyone who might be watching. He looked quickly right and left and right again. Tensed. Poised. He scurried forward at a pace that was much more effective than it was dignified.

If he could only reach the safety of the Federal Building hallways now. . . .


"Early? You? Something must be wrong, Longarm," Henry said with a grin. The United States marshal's clerk was only trying to be pleasant, but Deputy Custis Long frowned and walked woodenly across the room to hang his Stetson on the coat rack. The tensions, the problems of trying to avoid confrontation, were wearing on him, stripping him of his usual cheerful good humor. The day hadn't yet begun and already he felt drained and out of sorts.

"Is Billy in yet?" he asked, Billy being U.S. Marshal William Vail, the man both Longarm and Henry worked for.

"Yes, but there's no need for you to report to him," Henry said. "I have your stuff here. Nice and easy, too, you'll be glad to hear. He said you asked for a rest after that last job, and you've got it. A few warrants to serve is all you have to do this week. And nothing further away than Englewood. Just like you wanted." Henry was smiling again.

Longarm grimaced in response to news that should have been good. And last week he would have thought this very good news indeed. He'd been walking a razor thin tightrope all too often of late, teetering precariously between mere danger and utter disaster. He'd been due for a slower change of pace, and Billy Vail had agreed with him. But that had been Friday. Now it was Monday morning. And now things had changed.

Henry extended a sheaf of warrants for Longarm to take.

"In a minute, Henry. I want to see Billy first."

Henry shrugged, obviously not minding. "There's nobody in there with him if you want to go on in, Longarm."

"Thanks."

Longarm paused at the closed door to Billy Vail's private office and for a change actually thought to knock and wait

3

for a response before he barged into the boss's office.

"You got to help me, Billy," he blurted out almost before the balding U.S. marshal had time to look up from his desk. "You got to give me an assignment out of town this week, dammit. You just got to." There was something in Longarm's voice that was approaching desperation, and the look in his eyes was that of a haunted and harried man. "You just *got* to, Billy."

# Chapter 2

"I thought . . ."

"I know what I said Friday, Billy, but please. I got to get outta Denver for a while. Just a week or so would do it. Please?"

The United States marshal, Denver District, Department of Justice, began to smile. But then he hadn't gotten where he was by being stupid. Far from it. "I know you better than to think it's any kind of problem you could stand up and fight back against, Longarm. Which means it pretty much has to be a woman you're trying to avoid. Now surely you don't think the workings of this office should be disrupted just to accommodate the whims of some busybody female, do you?"

"Billy!" There was a note of desperation in Longarm's voice now, which only broadened the smile on Billy Vail's round face.

"A lawsuit, Longarm? No," he answered his own question. "I don't think so. You'd accept service of a writ. So it isn't a paternity suit. What then?"

"It's just . . . I'd rather not talk about it if it's all the same t' you, boss."

"You're serious, aren't you?"

"Damn right I am. This woman . . . jeez, Billy, she's crazy, I tell you. Moon-barking loco. All I done . . . never mind what I done. Point is, I didn't hardly do nothing. An' now she's all set t' wrap me up an' tie me down. I mean, she's got a preacher trottin' along behind wherever she goes, settin' there all ready t' say the words, Billy. Damn fool female's been popping out from under bushes, leaping

5

outta doorways, shinnying down ropes practically. I swear, Billy, it's got so I don't feel safe trying t' take a leak. The damn woman's apt t' trap me in an outhouse if I don't find one that has a back door."

Vail was openly laughing before his best deputy was through with his woeful tale. "You stepped in it, Longarm."

Glumly Longarm nodded.

"And I hate to tell you this, but there isn't anything going on that you'd be interested in."

"Now, Billy . . ."

"I'm serious, Longarm. The only thing I have that needs working on right now is a silly beef down in southeastern Colorado between some cavalrymen and townspeople. And frankly I'm not even sure there's anything to it. It's on a complaint from Colonel Leadhead. And you know what those are likely to be."

Longarm nodded. The colonel's name was actually Ledbetter. The nickname that was prevalent for him throughout the marshal's office was not an affectionate one. Colonel Ledbetter, who was an army adjutant something-or-other and assistant this-and-that for southern Colorado, was known to be something of an asshole. And an excitable, inaccurate one at that. No one took his complaints very seriously any longer. Hadn't since the same panicking fellow demanded that the governor activate the state militia and send them racing to the rescue of a group of embattled regular army infantrymen. The militia galloped boldly away to "save" the men from a band of Ute warriors, and discovered that the only danger the regulars were facing at the time was the danger of contracting venereal diseases from certain Ute maidens in the band.

The most unfortunate part of that affair was that Colonel Leadhead hadn't learned anything from it. He was and remained an asshole of the first water.

"I was planning on sending young Crowley down there," Billy said.

John Crowley was a newly, and temporarily, appointed deputy. The appointment was a blatant political accommodation, the sort of thing Billy Vail generally resented having to do and only rarely agreed to go along with. In Crowley's case the marshal was willing to go with the flow and accede to the appointment only because the young man was bright and genuinely interested in becoming a peace officer. And a case inspired by Colonel Leadhead was likely to give him the flavor of experience without making him undergo the spice of real danger. Assigning a top hand like Longarm to that sort of thing would amount to driving a carpet tack with a sledge hammer.

"Billy, I'm asking you polite. Gimme that case and let Crowley serve the in-town warrants that Henry laid out for me. Please?"

"You really are serious."

"I am. I admit it. You want me t' beg, Billy?"

"Lord, no. I'd never hear the end of it if I tried to make you do that."

"Good. But I'm still asking, Billy. Lemme have Crowley's assignment. Please."

The marshal shook his head, but he gave in. He took a folder from a corner of his always tidy desk and shoved it toward Longarm. "All I know, deputy, is what's in that report from Leadhead. It doesn't sound like much, so all I need you to do is to show up down at this Cimarron City and make the army commander there . . . the Remount Service post is called Camp Good Enough, don't ask me why . . . just make the guy happy."

Longarm grinned. He was feeling up to grinning some now that he knew he was going to be able to get out of the city for a spell. "Appropriations time coming around, Billy?"

Vail didn't say anything. He didn't need to. Sometimes the realities of politics intruded regardless of a man's preferences.

Longarm accepted the folder from his boss and began to read through the scanty information Colonel Leadhead had provided.

# Chapter 3

Longarm crossed his boots at the ankles and grunted with satisfaction. A cheroot fresh from the tobacconist's humidor was tucked into the corner of his mouth, leaving its excellent flavors there, and there was a glowing warmth in his belly, the result of a shot of rye whiskey that he'd consumed a few moments ago. The southbound Denver and Rio Grande smoking car rocked and jolted gently over the roadbed, and the steel wheels of the undercarriage clicked across the rail joints with a swift and pleasant regularity. Each and every one of those clicks meant that he was another—he had to think for a moment to call the figure back to mind—sixty-six feet away from Denver. Thank goodness. Deputy Marshal Custis Long felt considerably better now than he had earlier.

And after all, why shouldn't he? He was out of town, undetected, as good as on a vacation, and yet he had government travel vouchers in his pocket to pay for his travel needs. Hell, it couldn't get much better than this.

Leadhead's complaint certainly sounded like it would be no more dangerous or burdensome than a stroll along Cherry Creek. According to the excitable colonel, the services of a deputy were needed to curtail a wave of civilian crime in the vicinity of this Camp Good Enough place, wherever that was. Longarm wasn't quite clear on that point. Adjacent to Cimarron City, the complaint said. Wherever *that* was. What with mining camps and trail towns and skinning camps and trading posts, hell, towns sprouted out of the ground quick as mushrooms popping up on a manure pile. And most of them died just about as quick as they grew. A fella couldn't hope to keep up with them all.

Anyway, according to Colonel Leadhead, the residents of this Cimarron City were messing with the soldiers from Camp Good Enough and had to be stopped. Nothing in the report said why it was that the army wasn't tending to the task itself, which they generally would've preferred to do. But then when it came to Colonel Ledbetter there wasn't any point in looking for sense or logic in anything the man did.

Not that Longarm was complaining. Not hardly.

He grunted again and drew long and deep of the cool, rich smoke from his cheroot. He pulled the reliable Ingersol watch from his vest pocket and checked the time. If the train was on schedule they should be slowing for the Pueblo station in another fifteen, twenty minutes. Longarm would leave the Denver and Rio Grande there and transfer to an eastbound Kansas and Pacific for the run out along the Arkansas River valley to Fort Lyons. He would check in with Leadhead there and get the rest of the information he needed before he completed this easy-as-pie assignment. At any time, other than when Congress was considering appropriations, Longarm knew, a beef by Colonel Ledbetter would get short shrift. But asshole or not, the man had friends in high places. So right now it was more important than usual that he be accommodated. On the other hand, right now Custis Long was more willing than normal to accommodate him.

In the meantime . . . he slouched low in the seat and tipped his Stetson forward over his eyes. Fifteen or twenty minutes was time enough for a catnap.

Yessir, rest and relaxation was something he could look forward to getting for the next few days, until Leadhead's complaint was looked into and everybody concerned was happy again.

It was just as well likely that Longarm didn't know how wrong he was about that.

# Chapter 4

Longarm hitched a ride on an ambulance to get from the Kansas and Pacific platform to the scattered collection of single-story wood structures that was Fort Lyons.

Fort Lyons would have seemed very much in place in Missouri or even Virginia. In rugged Colorado it looked like something of an anomaly. Its physical setting was a grove of cottonwood and elm and pecan trees ranged along the Arkansas River, some of the trees native to the site but others introduced by high-ranking officers. Or, more likely, by the wives of the higher-ranking officers who had been posted to Lyons over the years. Lyons was a place where the wives were welcomed for their contributions to the social flair available here. The grounds were tidy and neat and were kept that way by constant attention from the private soldiers who served in this largely administrative establishment. There was not a single stone or adobe building in sight, although the laundry, hospital and several other structures were made of sound and solid, and relatively fireproof, brick. The wooden buildings that were lined in orderly rows across the grounds were all painted a uniform shade of yellow-beige. A post garden flourished on the flats beside the river where the produce would benefit from a ready supply of subterranean water, and the small parade ground looked like it was mowed with mechanical devices rather than simply being trampled flat by the pounding of many feet. Lyons was the sort of posting that even the most fastidious—even foppish—career officer would relish. It lent a man's service record a frontier aura without all the inconveniences like filth or discomfort or danger.

Longarm had had occasion to visit Lyons before. He made his way to the post headquarters complex without having to ask for directions.

"Yes?" The corporal who sat at a desk enclosed within a picket fence arrangement in the outer office area eyed the civilian visitor with distaste and carefully refrained from adding the customary "sir" to that greeting.

"Deputy Marshal Custis Long to see Colonel Ledbetter, Corporal."

"Deputy?"

"Deputy United States marshal."

The soldier straightened in his chair and exhibited interest for the first time. This civilian, it seemed, outranked him. "Very good, sir. Wait there, sir. I'll not be a minute, sir."

Longarm helped himself to a seat and lighted a cheroot to enjoy while he waited. The corporal trotted off down a hallway that ran through the center of the headquarters building. The long, low structure was laid out in a series of office cubicles on either side of the hallway; all the offices were the same eight feet or so of width but the length varied with the rank and importance of the offices who occupied them. From past visits, Longarm recalled that the largest office, at the far end on the left, belonged to the post commander. The next largest, smaller by not more than six inches along the outside wall dimension, belonged to Leadhead. Longarm yawned and crossed his legs.

"This way, sir."

"Thank you, Corporal." He rose and trailed the corporal into the hallway, and down it, not a dozen paces, before the receptionist stopped and motioned Longarm into an office on the right.

"Captain Bellengrath will be with you in a moment, sir. You may be seated to wait for him."

Longarm raised an eyebrow.

"Please be seated, sir."

There wasn't any point in arguing with a corporal. Not in a rank-high place like Lyons where first lieutenants were regarded as flunkies. He took a seat like a good boy and did as he was told.

11

Within five minutes or so he was joined in the small office by a red-haired captain whose brass said he was in the quartermaster corps. "You're the marshal?" He sounded brusque and businesslike.

"Deputy marshal," Longarm amended.

"Colonel Ledbetter is busy at the moment. I am familiar with the, um, request placed with the Justice Department." Captain Bellengrath was no doubt a conscientious and dutiful officer. Even so he was unable to keep from exhibiting a hint of the distaste he obviously felt at the idea of the United States Army asking for assistance from a civilian agency like Justice. There was a tightening at the temples and a downturn to the corners of his mouth when he mentioned what Leadhead had gone and done.

"You say Lead . . . uh . . . Colonel Ledbetter is busy?"

"Extremely," Bellengrath confirmed.

Longarm grunted and placed the soggy butt of his cheroot into the corner of his jaw where he could chew on it. The busywork was enough to keep him from smiling. Through the window past Bellengrath's shoulder Longarm could see Leadhead making a fast retreat in the direction of the senior officers' mess. "In that case, Captain," he said, "I'm right glad you can help me figure out what I'm doing here." He permitted himself that smile now.

# Chapter 5

Longarm had six days in which to mull over the things Captain Bellengrath told him. And the things that the captain had not told him.

The six days were how long it took the army supply train—officially it was a train although it consisted of only three wagons, three drivers, and one overworked helper—to travel from Fort Lyons to Camp Good Enough. Bellengrath, no doubt at Leadhead's idiotic suggestion, had denied the federal officer use of an army horse for the journey, claiming that would have been a waste of government resources since there was a supply train already scheduled into Good Enough. Besides, he'd said, Camp Good Enough was the closest Remount Service location. And it was from the Remount Service that civilian employees like Deputy Long were authorized to draw saddle stock.

That was one of the things Bellengrath *had* said. Among the things he had not mentioned . . . Longarm wasn't too sure about. But he knew damned good and well there was more behind this request for law enforcement assistance than met the eye.

Officially, the United States marshal had been asked to quell unspecified disturbances among the civilian population in the vicinity of Camp Good Enough, i.e., at the town known as Cimarron City.

Period.

Everything else Longarm wanted to know he'd had to ask about specifically. And even then the answers had not been particularly forthcoming.

The post commander at Good Enough was Capt. Harold Denis.

Camp Good Enough was indeed a Remount point. It was also, however, charged with picket responsibilities at the extreme western end of the Unassigned Lands of the Indian Territories, guarding against any reservation breakouts or depredation raids by the wild tribes that were supposed to be confined on the I.T. And in addition to that the soldiers of Good Enough were supposed to police activities along the Ogallala Trail, the trail drovers' road established by the federal government along the Kansas/Colorado border so the herds of cattle being moved north from Texas could bypass the settled farm country further to the east and keep from bringing dreaded tick fever with them.

Cimarron City took its name from the Cimarron River. Bellengrath, despite whatever unpleasant instructions he might have been given by Leadhead, had been forced to smile about that one. Yes, he'd agreed when Longarm questioned that. If the damned town had been built on the banks of the Cimarron it would have been in New Mexico Territory or in Texas or just possibly in the Indian Territories. But no, it couldn't be situated on the Cimarron and be in Colorado. The simple fact was, whoever named the place may have thought he was standing beside the Cimarron but he damn sure was not. Instead, Cimarron City was sited beside a creek known on the government survey maps by the scintillating title Big Skull Wash.

"Big skull found there? Or a big wash?" Longarm'd asked.

Bellengrath had only been able to shrug and shake his head. "Your guess would be as good as mine about that."

Not that it mattered either way. Longarm's only interest was how he could go about finding Camp Good Enough and Cimarron City. And all he had to do to accomplish that was to sit on his butt for six days while the army supply train rattled and bumped southeast out of Fort Lyons across mile after endless mile of rolling, sparsely grassed plains with rarely so much as a good sized rock in sight to break the visual monotony.

By the time they got there he was so butt-sore and bored that he was pleased to see anything, even a place as dreary and unpleasant as Camp Good Enough.

# Chapter 6

Dreary? That was putting it in the kindest and most charitable way possible.

Ah hell, it could've been worse, Longarm conceded as he stood on the caprock bluff overlooking the valley of Big Skull Wash and peered down at Camp Good Enough and, a mile or so west of the army post, Cimarron City.

The civilian teamster in charge of the wagon train, a man named Vickery, spat a stream of brown juice into the dark, damp stain where he'd just relieved himself, buttoned his fly, and turned to face the tall deputy who had been his guest for the duration of the trip down from Fort Lyons. "Ever see a poorer post than this?" he asked.

"Yeah, I expect I have," Longarm told him, neglecting to add that it had been a while. "How long has this'un been here?"

"Six months or thereabouts," Vickery said.

"Hardly time enough to get much done then," Longarm excused. Although the truth was that damn little seemed to have been accomplished in six months' time. Camp Good Enough consisted of untidy rows of canvas tenting draped over low sod walls, latrine sinks that were walled but not roofed, a flagpole that a man on horseback could probably touch the top of, and a short picket line where a handful of horses were tied.

There was no headquarters building that Longarm could see. No hospital, no laundry, no stables, no barracks, and, the oddest lack of all on a Remount post, no corrals or training pens.

Not only did none of those things exist, none of them

15

seemed to be under construction yet.

Longarm shrugged and lighted a cheroot for himself, turning his attention to the town that lay a mile or so upstream along Big Skull Wash.

Cimarron City was slightly larger and seemingly more prosperous than the army camp. At least its buildings had been erected with some degree of permanence in mind. They were of stone and sod for the most part, but many of the businesses fronting on the main street had two-story tall false fronts to show off with. The business district consisted of an unbroken stretch of buildings that would be, he guessed, the equivalent of two or two and a half city blocks in Denver. There was also a scattering of shacks and small houses sprouting here, there, and everywhere in a random pattern surrounding the town district.

For such an isolated area, the town street showed a good amount of traffic. Longarm guessed that the merchants here would draw trade from ranches situated within a hundred miles or so, from freighters detouring in off the old Cimarron Cut-off of the Santa Fe Trail, from cattle drovers on the Ogallala, from homesteaders who hadn't yet starved off their dry land farms . . . and of course, first and foremost, from the soldiers newly assigned to Camp Good Enough. Virtually every army post quickly generates a town within sight of its walls, if only because soldiers have the most secure paydays of anybody and can be counted on to spend their meager earnings as quickly as they pocket the money. Saloons, whorehouses and cafés where something other than bland and boring army food can be bought are *always* to be found within a stone's throw of an army camp.

Longarm guessed that Cimarron City would have begun in much that way and then expanded to meet other opportunities as they might have been found here.

"I reckon the horses are rested enough now, Mr. Long," Vickery said. "We can start down now if you're ready." Six days and Longarm hadn't yet convinced Vickery to call him anything other than Mr. Long, which was how Bellengrath's corporal had introduced them back at Fort Lyons. Vickery hadn't really unburdened himself enough to allow much in the way of companionship either, and he'd kept his employees at arm's length, too. Longarm had long since determined that Vickery either knew nothing about the problems down here . . . or professed to know nothing. Whatever the truth, he was willing to offer no opinions on any subject relating to Camp Good Enough or Cimarron City.

"Ready when you are, Mr. Vickery." They walked together to Vickery's tall wagon and made the six-foot climb onto the driving box. The teamster took up a light bit contact with the driving lines and eased his team forward and gently onto the breechin' straps as the path angled sharply downhill. Whatever else Vickery might be, the man was an excellent driver.

"It ain't all dry and ugly here, Mr. Long, as you can see for yourself now if you care to look around to your right," Vickery ventured when they were about halfway down the bluff face.

Longarm looked in the direction indicated. Now he could see something that previously was hidden behind a jutting point of rock. On the top of the bluff, towering high above them from this vantage point, there was a house.

Not some drab and tiny little bit of the thing like were clustered around the business district of Cimarron City, though. This was a HOUSE.

Three stories tall, with dormer windows and porches on the lower two floors and glass in the window frames reflecting copper and gold in the light of a slanting afternoon sun. Smoke curled out of the rearwardmost of three tall chimneys.

Longarm could see that someone had even gone to the trouble to plant tall, young saplings in a someday grove around three sides of the house, leaving only the front free so the residents there would be able to sit on their porches and look out across the miles and miles of rolling prairie while the trees would serve as shade and windbreak shelter when, or if, they grew to maturity. The likelihood of them reaching full growth was in doubt, Longarm knew, because it would take much patience and careful watering to bring trees to maturity on a high, exposed location like that bluff-top site.

Still and all, if someone had that much patience and took that much effort he would be amply rewarded ten or twenty years hence.

"A place like that hasn't popped up in any six months," Longarm said.

"No sir, they say the colonel has been here for years an' years," Vickery said.

"Colonel?"

"It's what he's called. Never heard what he's supposed to've been a colonel of, though. Union army, o' course. I mean, the man's name is Sherman. Rumor has it that he's some sort of kin to General Sherman. But I wouldn't know about that. Just that he's been here a helluva lot longer than that army camp over there or the town, either one. I know that an' that the colonel, he don't socialize with nobody from post or town neither one."

"I see," Longarm said, not particularly caring whether this sometime colonel was a sociable sort or not. His business had nothing to do with eccentrics who chose to build grand manor houses in unlikely locations. He turned his concentration instead on Camp Good Enough where it properly belonged.

"Half an hour, Mr. Long, and I'll have you safely delivered." The teamster sounded more than a little relieved at the prospect of being shut of the deputy after all this time.

"Thank you, Mr. Vickery."

# Chapter 7

Now wasn't *that* interesting, Longarm mused as Vickery's wagons rolled the last few rods into Good Enough. What the hell had they thought, that he wouldn't come down here if he knew? Or did the officers at Fort Lyons genuinely believe there wasn't anything worth mentioning about the troops here?

Longarm knew the answer to that one right enough. That asshole Leadhead thought he'd gone and pulled a fast one, thought he'd managed to take a shitty job off the U.S. Army's shoulders and lay it onto the Justice Department.

What Colonel Ledbetter didn't know—and likely wouldn't have believed even if he'd been told—was that the United States Justice Department, and U.S. Marshal William Vail after them, and in particular Deputy Marshal Custis Long, honestly didn't give a damn. It would've been the same to all of them regardless.

Longarm shook his head, more amused by Leadhead's stupid attempt at deception than bothered by it.

The thing was, the troops here at Good Enough were Negro soldiers.

Leadhead and his fancypants parade ground officers hadn't wanted to put themselves in the position of defying white settlers on behalf of colored troops. Custis Long didn't happen to care much about that. Not either way. He wasn't no bleeding heart, and he wasn't going to make his decisions on the basis of anything as shallow as that. It was the right and the wrong of a thing that interested him. None of the rest of it was worth bothering with. But it seemed that wasn't an opinion that was shared by Leadhead and those other idiots at Lyons.

Longarm chuckled a mite and then settled back on the driving seat of Vickery's lead wagon. He crossed his boots at the ankles and lighted a cheroot, feeling considerably relieved now that he understood the things Bellengrath hadn't been willing to tell him back there at the fort. Why hell, if this was all they'd been worried about . . .

Vickery dropped Longarm off at the headquarters tent, then took his wagons and rumbled off about his business.

Longarm deposited his carpetbag beside a white painted signpost—the sign on it read: 3rd Battalion, 745th Infantry (Colored)—and ducked to pass through the tent flap on his way inside.

"Ten-SHUN!" There was a rustle and clatter as a handful of enlisted men in the front portion of the big tent snapped to rigid attention.

Longarm blinked and gave them a sheepish look. "I, uh, I'm not an officer. No need for this. Sorry."

"At ease," barked a sergeant standing behind a field desk. The other soldiers relaxed so little it was hard to see that they'd relaxed at all. They did, however, resume their seats. None actually went back to whatever he'd been doing before Longarm walked in. They did not bother to pretend that they weren't watching him closely. Longarm felt like he was all of a sudden on stage. On all sides there were dark faces and wide eyes turned toward him.

"Would you mind telling Captain Denis he has a visitor, Sergeant?" Longarm asked of the man who seemed to be in charge.

"Your name and the nature of your complaint, sir?" The sergeant, a middle-aged man with skin the color of a trail cook's coffee and a set of three rockers to balance his three chevrons, took up a pencil and notepad. His voice was crisp and businesslike.

Longarm smiled. "No complaint, Sergeant. Deputy Marshal Long to see Captain Denis. That's all."

"Yes, sir." The first sergeant jotted something on the notepad. "Your jurisdiction, Deputy? And if you don't mind . . . it would save time, sir . . . the name of the man you've come to arrest?"

Longarm frowned. "Sergeant, I don't think you and me are talking about the same things here. I . . ."

"Please, sir, this is not new to us. Captain Denis likes things done in a certain way, sir. If you do not mind, sir . . ."

"Sergeant, I'm still not getting through t' you, am I? My name is Custis Long. I am a deputy United States marshal. An' I haven't come here to arrest *any*body. Okay? No warrants. No beefs. No big deal. All right? For right now all I want is to have a talk with Captain Denis. Am I making myself clear now?"

It was the first sergeant's turn to frown. He glanced toward a corporal who was seated at another desk, then back at Longarm. "As you wish, sir." The corporal got up and wandered outside as if he hadn't a care in the world. Longarm suppressed a smile. These soldiers, he suspected, were protecting their own. By the time Deputy Long got in to see Captain Denis there would be an ear pressed to the canvas close by. Whatever Longarm said to the Camp Good Enough commander would be relayed to the first sergeant in short order. And in truth Longarm had no quarrel with that. It could mean that the top level noncoms of the outfit were sharp and were protecting their unit and their officers. There were other things it could mean, too, reasons not as positive as the protection of one's unit or one's officers. But Longarm wasn't willing to assume any of those things. Not until or unless he had cause. He waited while the first sergeant fiddled with some papers on his desk—and while the corporal got within eavesdropping distance—then followed the sergeant through the headquarters to a separate, smaller tent set immediately to the rear.

"Wait here a moment, sir." The first sergeant let himself into Captain Denis's office and was back in a moment as promised. "The captain will see you now, sir."

Capt. Harold Denis was typical of the postwar period, typical of the problems that Longarm expected would plague the military through the end of the century and perhaps beyond.

Too many men had achieved high rank during the course of the War Between the States. And too many of those men remained in uniform when the war was over and the army was shrinking back to a peacetime size.

There were many more officers than were really needed for the available jobs, and networks of friendships and political obligations kept the dead wood from being pruned away as it really should have been.

There were a great many consequences resulting from this oversupply of commissioned officers. One of them was that promotion was almost impossible to come by even for the very best officers remaining on active duty. Men who by virtue of age and experience would ordinarily have been full colonels, perhaps even general officers, found themselves reaching retirement age with only a major's boards on their shoulders. And then these people compounded their own problems by remaining in service for years, even decades, longer than they should have simply so they could try to reach a respectable rank and level of retirement pay before they finally hung their uniforms away.

Army Captain Harold Denis was at least in his late fifties and probably was in his early sixties. He might well have been serving his country for the past forty years. And he was only a captain, spending his final years commanding an understrength colored battalion on the fringes of nowhere.

It was a damned shame, Longarm realized. And it was entirely typical nowadays. Longarm wouldn't have blamed Denis if he'd been bitter and wrapped himself in misery or perhaps tried to hide inside a whiskey bottle as so many hopeless career officers attempted.

Instead, Captain Denis looked up with a sun-bright smile of welcome. His uniform was clean and impeccably tailored. His collar was crisp and tidy. His eyes were sparkling clear.

"A rarity," he declared pleasantly when he saw Longarm. "A great rarity indeed, my sergeant tells me, sir. A civilian who has no quarrel here. An officer of the law who has not come to arrest one of my men. Welcome, Deputy. Welcome to Camp Good Enough."

# Chapter 8

"There isn't anything going on here that my troops and I couldn't handle by ourselves," Captain Denis said once the pleasantries had been dispensed with and they were able to get down to business.

"Really?" Longarm crossed his legs and leaned back. He had a cheroot locked in the corner of his jaw. Its twin lay in Captain Denis's fist, a thin stream of white smoke rising toward the canvas roof now.

Denis smiled, the expression tight but not at all grim. He seemed to be genuinely enjoying having company. "One of the advantages for a man in my otherwise unenviable position, Marshal, is that I have nothing left to lose. Careerwise, that is. I mean, I no longer harbor false hopes about promotion or glory. I'll draw my pay until they force me out. Then I'll draw somewhat less. But they can't take away what little I have. Not at this late date." He chuckled. "I might not have many friends at court who would have seen to my advancement, Deputy, but I've been blessed with a fair number of enemies. And fortunately I know where my enemies have buried the bodies. Figuratively speaking, that is. So what little I have is secure. I don't have to mince words, you see, or pretend for the sake of appearances."

Longarm decided he just might learn to like this overaged captain of infantry.

"They stuck me out here at the ends of the earth in the hope that I'd give up and turn in my retirement papers," Denis said. "Then to make it all the worse, you see, they saddled me with the dregs of the department when it comes to my officers, no sense trying to pretend that that isn't so, and of course a batch of Negroes to serve as my garrison troops. Ha. Why, those idiots back in St. Louis don't have any idea about the quality of manpower they have out here. These soldiers are among the best I've ever seen. Certainly they are the finest I've ever been privileged to command. But would anyone at headquarters be capable of understanding that? I think not. The point, anyway, is that in sending me out here to stagnate they've gone and done me the kindest favor I've ever received by way of an assignment. Wonderfully dedicated men under my command here, I tell you. Men who have to work three times as hard as white troops simply to be accepted as the most ordinary of soldiers. Excellent noncoms. Spit and polish in the lowest ranks. And a quarter of the disciplinary problems of any other outfit I've ever seen. These men are here because they want to be. They take pride in their uniforms, you see." Denis drew on the cheroot Longarm had given him and leaned forward. "You don't seem uncomfortable about hearing this, Deputy."

Longarm shook his head. "Not surprised either, Captain. I've seen the Buffalo Soldiers at work. If your infantry is as good as those boys then you've got a fine outfit here."

"I'll be damned. Usually . . . well, you can guess what my enthusiasm usually returns."

Longarm shrugged. "Everybody has his own prejudices, Captain. Including you and me. This colored unit just doesn't happen t' hit any o' mine."

"And yours might be . . . ?" Denis prompted.

The tall deputy grinned and shifted in his chair. "Stupidity irks me. So does meanness. I'm right firm in my prejudices against them things, Captain."

Denis snorted and nodded his head in agreement. "Good on you, deputy. Good on you."

"Y'know, Captain, my friends mostly call me Longarm."

"Very good, Longarm. And you shall call me Hal."

"Fair 'nough, Hal."

"As I was saying before, Longarm, there isn't anything going on here that these men and I couldn't handle. If only those fools at Fort Lyons would allow us to handle it. But they're in a panic lest a bunch of niggers impose order on white civilians. Never mind that my troops are the ones in the right here. That makes no difference. The gentlemen . . . and I call them that only because the Congress of these United States claims that they are officers and therefore gentlemen . . . are so concerned about appearances and possible political repercussions that right and wrong are left to sort themselves out. Hence the request that a federal law officer come down and look into it. And frankly I doubt they would have bothered to ask that the disturbances be halted except that it wouldn't look good on their records if men under their command wind up murdered without anything being done about it."

"Murder?" Longarm asked, sitting upright on his chair now. "This is the first I've heard anything 'bout murder, Hal."

"No, no, Longarm. No one has been murdered. Not yet. But it would be only a matter of time if this business were allowed to get out of hand. I'm convinced of that."

Longarm relaxed a little. "Nobody has yet got around to telling me much about the situation over at Cimarron City, Hal."

"The usual," Denis said. "They want my boys' pay over there. They just don't want to put up with the men while their money is being spent. My troops have learned to walk in twos or threes when they go into town. Even so they have to suffer attacks. Fist fights, rocks thrown at them from the shadows, that sort of thing. Separate facilities in all things, naturally. My men understand that and seem not to resent it. Although I have to believe that they really do. They are entitled to resentment over it. But that sort of thing is only to be expected. What worried me enough to plan a campaign of, um, correction . . . which was overruled by Colonel Ledbetter, by the way, and led to the request that brought you here . . . is the escalation of ugliness that has been taking place. Random shootings at night. Once that began I became worried."

"You said no one has been murdered, but now you mention shootings," Longarm pointed out.

"No one has died yet. None of my people, that is. But two of my men have been wounded, neither seriously, thank goodness. And there was at least one civilian death. A white woman, a rather old and tawdry whore, was found hanged. It was officially ruled a suicide, which of course is entirely common among that class of female, but my men dispute the verdict. They say she was hanged by a vigilance committee because she'd begun accepting my men as, uh, customers. She hadn't been able to make a living selling herself for fifty cents to whites, but she was able to earn a dollar from my blacks. And had much more trade as well." Denis shrugged. "Frankly I'm no expert in that area, Longarm. I only know that my men believe the woman was murdered by these vigilantes. If so, if such a group really has been formed in Cimarron City, then I fear the area faces some difficult times ahead. I would have handled it myself if I had been allowed to do so, you understand. And I am convinced I could have quelled the problem. A company of men with bayonets fixed and the drums beating, everyone moving in precision drill, I daresay it is a sight that can have a chilling effect on nearly any ordinary opposition. Including a committee of vigilance."

"I wouldn't bet against that," Longarm agreed.

"A moot point now, of course. Colonel Ledbetter in his wisdom felt it better to invite you here." Denis smiled and lightened up. "Now that you are here, Longarm, why, I am glad it worked out this way. The same ends will be accomplished, and I shall have the pleasure of having you as my guest in the officers' mess as well, eh?"

"The pleasure'll be mine, Hal."

"And if there is any way we can assist you here, anything whatsoever, all you need do is name it. We will be glad to see to it."

"This is s'posed t' be a Remount point," Longarm said, "so I'd like t' draw a horse. If you got some, that is."

Denis laughed. "I can understand your confusion, Longarm. But we do have Remount facilities. You didn't see them when you arrived because we've placed all of that downstream on a broad flat where the grazing is good. The site is about two miles away and can't be seen from here. We have our stables, corrals, the horse herd itself, all the Remount-related facilities down there. That is where all our construction efforts have been expended so far.

26

The men have had to suffer these first few months so the horses won't have to once winter sets in. Fortunately the men understand that their government regards a horse as being of more value than a soldier." The officer chuckled again. But Longarm knew that he was being quite serious about that. In the army, horses and mules do take precedence over private soldiers.

Longarm stood.

"You aren't leaving already, are you?" Denis sounded disappointed, as if he'd been looking forward to plenty more conversation with this newfound friend. But then Longarm recalled that the captain had openly admitted that his junior officers at Good Enough were the dregs of the department. And it was no secret that the civilians at Cimarron City resented having the army here. Probably Capt. Harold Denis had no one to converse with for months at a time. No wonder the man wanted Longarm to stay.

"I need to borrow that horse off your people, Hal, and then get over t' the town for a spell. I need t' have a closer look at it. But I'll be back an' we can talk more then. Count on it."

"I take that as a promise, Longarm."

"An' so it is, Hal."

"Wait a moment and I'll go with you. I want to issue orders about that horse you need." The captain stood and made his way around to the front of his desk, then on toward the front. There hadn't been anything to give his disabilities away when he was seated, but now Longarm could see that Denis had one leg that was stiff and seemed shorter than the other. He limped badly but moved swiftly enough and without obvious pain. An old wound suffered in the line of duty? Denis didn't say and Longarm certainly didn't ask.

By the time Longarm and the post commander reached the front portion of the headquarters tent, the corporal who'd been sent to monitor the conversation was already there, bending to the first sergeant's ear in animated conversation. The enlisted men in the reception area snapped to rigid attention at the appearance of their commander. Everything by the book, everything by the numbers. Longarm was reminded, somehow, of the eagerness of a good gundog on point. Well,

Denis had said his troops were sharp. If these men weren't then they managed one helluva imitation of it.

Captain Denis issued orders that the deputy was to receive full cooperation from all personnel and passed along the request that a mount be provided immediately. "See that the order is logged in the daybook, Sergeant Prior."

"Yes, sir." The first sergeant's voice was as crisp as an October morning.

"You have an open invitation to join me in the mess, Longarm," Denis said before he offered his hand. "See that you use it."

"First chance I get, Hal," he promised. Longarm shook hands with the army captain, then followed the first sergeant outside. A handsome bay gelding was waiting there, Longarm's own saddle and gear already in place on its back.

"Anything you need, sir, you let me know. No matter what it is," Sergeant Prior offered as Longarm was swinging onto the bay. That was what he'd been ordered by his officer, of course. But there was something in the first sergeant's voice that made Longarm think there was more than military compliance in the offer.

"Thank you, Sergeant. Thank you very much." Longarm reined the sleek and leggy bay toward Cimarron City. Why shucks, if he got as much cooperation there as he was getting at Good Enough . . .

# Chapter 9

It had been quite a while since Longarm last sat a horse that moved as nice or felt as good as the Remount bay did. Whoever picked this one knew what he was doing. And whoever it was who'd ordered it saddled for the civilian visitor was one almighty kind and generous soul. Longarm put the horse into a rocking chair lope for the short ride over to the town.

It was late afternoon when he first rode down the single street that comprised the business district of Cimarron City. A wagon park at the near end of town was filled with freight rigs. Including, he thought, the now empty wagons that Vickery had brought down from Fort Lyons.

Considering that, and that he was on a U.S.-branded horse, there was no chance he could pass himself off here as anything but who and what he really was.

Not that he'd had inclinations in that direction. It likely would have been a waste of time and effort to bother sliding undercover for a case so simple as this one oughta be. It was just that the option wasn't open to him this time.

Longarm pulled rein in front of a saloon chosen at random—small as the town was there were nevertheless so many to pick from that it would've been difficult to try and work out a sensible choice—and led the bay to a post-mounted hitching ring there.

A middle-aged man wearing lace-up boots and a grease-stained red flannel shirt ambled close and gave first the bay and then Longarm a critical inspection. "Huh," he grunted. He made a face like he'd just smelled something foul and spat on the board sidewalk. "It ain't gonna work," he declared.

The man had a chest that resembled a beer barrel. And a gut that looked like it could hold a barrel of beer. His hands were thick and his jowls beefy. He looked like you could use his face for an anvil and not succeed in making him blink.

"Pardon me?" Longarm inquired.

"I said it ain't gonna work, sonny."

"Am I supposed t' know what you mean by that, friend?"

"You know, I reckon. An' don't you be callin' me that ag'in. I ain't no friend o' yours now an' I ain't fixing to be later. Fact is, I think all you so'jer boys is a bunch o' pricks. So don' call me that ag'in or I'll beat the shit outta you. In fact, I jus' might go an' beat the shit outta you anyhow."

"If you say so," Longarm told him mildly. He finished tying the horse to the hitching ring and stepped wide around the belligerent townsman.

"Smartass son of a bitch," the man snarled behind his back.

Longarm stopped where he was.

"Think we don't know what you are, bluebelly? Think just 'cause you ride in wearin' c'vilian clothes we won't know ye? Shit. You're a damn ossifer."

"Or else the whitest looking nigger they got in that nest of 'em," another townsman said.

Longarm saw now that several passersby had slowed and were stopping, attracted to this quiet sidewalk confrontation by whatever process it is that signals blood and draws men to the sight of it.

The local man's quip brought a roar of laughter from the suddenly growing crowd. And that loud laughter turned heads further away down the street. Soon there was a general drift from all directions, men filtering nearer and the size of the crowd growing quickly larger.

"Which is it, sonny?" the first man demanded. "A ossifer? Or a albino nigger?" For some reason he and his pals all seemed to think the question hilarious.

Longarm scowled. But turned away from the confrontation. "Excuse me, please. Excuse me? Would you move there, please, I'd like to get through." He was surrounded now. The burly man in the red shirt was directly in front of him. Crowding him. Egged on by the attention of the crowd around them now.

"Where you think you're goin', boy? Jus' where d'you think you're goin'?"

"Yella son of a bitch," someone in the crowd shouted.

"The officer is a fuckin' coward," another voice prodded.

"Takes after them nigger so'jers," someone else yelled.

"Teach 'im how to fight, Charley." "Teach him to come sneaking around here pretending to be as good as a white man, Charley." "Give him something to take back with him, Charley." "Yeah, Charley, give him some bruises to take back." "Break his fucking head open, Charley."

"Nice folks you got around here, Charley," Longarm observed.

"Turn an' run so'jer boy. Go ahead. We'll let ya." The big man called Charley cackled and taunted.

Turn and run was good advice under these circumstances. It was the sensible thing to do. Hell, these fellows were just feeling petty and mean and the fact that a crowd had gathered was putting all of them on their worst behavior. The proper and sensible thing for him to do would be to turn around now and get back on that bay horse and trot back over to Good Enough. Hal Denis would probably be heading for the officers' mess soon. Longarm could join him there and make his presence known in Cimarron City tomorrow when things would be calmer.

That would be the sensible thing.

But dammit, it would also make a coward of him before these townspeople. And a peace officer can't allow that to happen. Not ever. Because that is when the idiots and the assholes feel they have to test it, push to the limit and then beyond. No, dammit, Longarm's sense of duty wouldn't allow that to happen.

Or so he rationalized to himself.

The real story was that he was becoming pissed off with these yahoos. With Charley in particular and with all the fool's friends in general.

And turning around and meekly going back over to Camp Good Enough simply wasn't what Deputy Marshal Custis Long had in mind at this moment.

Longarm smiled. "Charley, old friend," he said gently. "Whyn't you an' me clear ourselves a little space so's we can commence to snap assholes at one another? Hmm? Or are you as yellow as you are fat?"

The big man called Charley reached a nice, rich shade of purple once that sank in.

By that time Longarm had his coat and gunbelt off and was standing in the middle of the street waiting for the SOB.

# Chapter 10

Longarm was hoping that ol' Charley was one of those unschooled bullies who has always been able to rely on brute strength to gain his victories and therefore is a sucker for a man who knows what he is doing with the fine and delicate art of rough-and-tumble.

Longarm was shit outta luck.

Charley came on for those first few steps in a bull-like rush. But long before he came within striking range of Longarm's ready fists the man stopped, hunched into a fighting crouch and set himself into a modified version of the Marquis of Queensbury stance.

This guy wasn't just big. He also knew what he was doing.

Longarm suppressed the groan that dang near slipped out. But it wasn't easy.

"Well, so'jer boy?" Charley taunted.

"It's your game, friend. You call the rules," Longarm returned. Charley had gone into a fighter's crouch. Longarm simply stood there and looked at him.

"No rules," Charley said. "We go till one of us . . . me . . . gets tired o' beating on the other. Which'll be you." The beefy man grinned, exposing teeth that were much too white and pretty to be his own.

"Your choice," Longarm said agreeably. He pointed over toward the bay where his coat and hat and gunbelt were balanced atop his saddle. "Want to get rid of anything first, Charley? Your teeth maybe? Be a damn shame t' bust 'em."

"I ain't worried 'bout it, so'jer boy. An' I warned you a'ready. Don't you be calling me your friend, because I damn sure ain't one."

"Charley, you amaze me. If I make you mad by doing that, what're you gonna do about it, hmm? Fight me? Shit, you're already doing that."

Charley laughed, his dark eyes sparkling with quick humor at that reminder. "You got a point there," he conceded. It occurred to Longarm that under other circumstances this Charley might not be such a bad sort of fella.

But that would've been under circumstances decidedly different from the facts of the here and the now. No point in thinking about any of that now.

"So, friend. What'll it be?" Longarm asked.

"This." Charley feinted a left jab, right hook combination that Longarm easily ducked away from.

Which, unfortunately, was precisely what Charley intended.

Longarm's sideways dart to slide away from the punches positioned him nicely for the snake-quick kick that apparently had been Charley's goal from the outset of that little maneuver.

Like probably countless opponents before him, Longarm was suckered into believing that Charley's bulky build, his massive shoulders, and thick arms indicated a puncher.

In fact the man was as light on his feet as a dancer, and was even quicker.

He leaped into the air with a shout, and one tall, lace-up boot came snapping toward Longarm's jaw like a bolt of brown lightning. If the kick had landed the fight would have been over there and then. And Longarm would have had a broken jaw as a souvenir at the very least.

Instead Longarm swayed back at the waist and jerked his head to the side in a reflexive reaction. Charley's boot swept by close enough that Longarm could feel the wind of its passage wash softly over his cheek and could smell the drying manure that Charley had stepped in right recently.

Even as he was pulling aside from the unexpected kick Longarm was countering it with a rising chop of his right forearm. He caught Charley's extended leg behind the ankle and lifted it, using the momentum of the man's own kick and carrying that to an illogical extreme that dumped Charley onto his back with one leg extended high in the air.

34

Charley hit the ground hard enough to drive the breath from him. But not hard enough to slow him down or to make him quit thinking.

Before Longarm had time to jump clear, Charley was kicking with his other leg, the kick sweeping in behind Longarm's knee and toppling him.

Longarm felt himself begin to fall. The natural reaction would be to try and fight against the fall. Instead he went with it, throwing himself in the direction his weight was already moving and taking advantage of the motion to fling himself clear of Charley's too-dangerous boots. Longarm let himself fall, his own leap turning the movement into a rolling dive that carried him out of the middle of the street where this had begun and on toward the hitching rails and the crowd that was gathered behind them.

He hadn't had time to actually plan where he was going to end up. Or he might have done things somewhat different.

As it was he ended up on all fours with his head tucked underneath the fuzzy belly of a grulla mare—she was damn sure a mare as he was in a good position to see, his head at that particular moment in time being butted hard into her udder. She acted like she wasn't much used to the notion of having humans wallow about on the ground under her feet. Her ears pinned tight against her skull and her teeth bared, she squealed and commenced to fidget.

Longarm scurried on in the direction he was already pointing, clearing out from underneath the mare just about the time ol' Charley—for just about half a second there Longarm had actually forgotten about friend Charley—came after him with another hard, snapping kick.

There was a name for this kicking style of fighting. A real name that is, other than simply skunk-mean or whatever. Longarm couldn't think of it at that moment, but he knew there was one. His big question right now wasn't what to call it but what the fuck to do about it. Charley was pressing his attack so quick Longarm hadn't yet had a chance to set himself and try to get in some licks of his own.

On the other hand, ol' Charley wasn't accomplishing a helluva lot yet either.

This time Longarm slid out from under the grulla mare just ahead of Charley's next kick.

That'un was one hellacious kick, though. Longarm could tell that it was by the sound the mare made when Charley's boot sank into her belly. The air whooshed out of her in a loud rush.

The mare was already pissed off by Longarm's intrusions on her privacy. Her ears were already pinned and her dander was already up.

She snorted and blew snot over the crowd, then humped up in the middle and kicked back at the human thing that'd gone and kicked at her.

There was something of a lesson to be learned there. Folks might learn how to kick. But horses have a sort of natural talent for it.

The grulla mare's kick landed flush on Charley's chest and flipped him onto his back in the dirt.

Any halfway sensible man, Longarm knew, would let it go at that. Or if he was real persistent might jump up and run around behind the mare so he could get after his human opponent once again.

Ol' Charley seemed to've gone beyond clear thinking in the last minute or so, his brain filled with the red roar of a good fight or something.

For whatever reason, though, the guy bounced up and came boring right on in the same direction once again.

Except this time he was prepared for that damned mare. This time he kicked first. Charley kicked the grulla like he was fixing to boot it plumb out of the way and clear the path between him and Longarm.

Charley's boot landed in the neighborhood of that mare's near stifle.

Which she did not appreciate.

She kicked Charley in the belly.

Charley staggered, set himself and kicked the mare in the butt.

The mare retaliated with a squeal and a stamping of her forefeet and a hard, two-hoofed high shot that barely missed Charley's head.

Charley kicked the horse again. The guy was obviously

so pissed off right now that he wasn't much caring who or what he was kicking.

The horse kicked Charley again.

Longarm leaned against the rump of his Remount bay and propped his chin on his elbow, feigning a yawn as he watched the show. Nobody in the crowd seemed to mind the changes that'd taken place in the public tussle. Most of them seemed to be rooting for the mare now.

"Damn you," Charley grunted. He launched his right boot at the tender spot just at the base of the mare's tail.

He was unlucky enough to hit what he was aiming at.

Mad? The grulla acted like she'd been playing up till then. Now she was purely peeved.

She bogged her head and let out a high-pitched whistle of marrow-deep mad, then tattooed Charley's middle with a flurry of hoofs that flew too hard and too fast for mortal man to count.

Charley ended up lying on his back in the center of the street. The plunging, lunging mare ended up on the sidewalk with a chunk of busted hitch rail hanging from her reins. Men scattered, most of them to get out of the way of the enraged grulla, a few chasing after the horses she'd loosed when her shenanigans broke the rail.

Longarm glanced to make sure his bay was still secure on the post-mounted ring where he'd tied it, then wandered out into the street and held a hand down for Charley to grab hold of.

"Unless you'd ruther lay there a spell," he suggested.

"Jeez," Charley said.

"Ain't that the truth."

The big man grinned. "I done some dumb things in my time. But that'un was a corker."

Longarm laughed. "C'mon, friend. I'll buy you a beer. It occurs t' me that you'll be needing one about now."

Charley laughed, too, and let Longarm pull him to his feet. He winced once he was upright, pressing his hand to a midsection that was undoubtedly sore already. And would be sorer yet once it had time to draw tight. "Damn," he mumbled. He cocked his head in Longarm's direction and, squinting, said, "I never been whupped by a so'jer boy. You won't mind if I mark this down t' the horse an' not you, will you?"

"Won't mind at all," Longarm assured him. "An' even if I was to whup you, friend, it wouldn't spoil that record. I ain't no soldier boy."

"No? Why in hell didn' you say so?"

"Nobody bothered t' ask."

"I'll be damn."

Longarm grinned and introduced himself.

"No shit?"

"No shit, Charley."

Charley decided that was a good one on him. He called out for everybody to hear how badly he'd been fooled, then completed introductions all around as best he could. Longarm guessed that at least half the male population of Cimarron City must have been on hand for the fistfight that never quite happened.

"C'mon, boys," Charley announced. "Me an' my new friend Longarm are buying."

Which was a popular announcement indeed. It was Longarm's turn to wince. On the other hand, well, if he could somehow convince Henry that this expenditure was being made in the line of duty . . .

"That's right, boys. The beer is on us." Beer, dammit, not the good stuff. There were limits to generosity even when the open-handed party was Uncle Sam.

The grulla mare, he noticed, had been tied at the next rail over now, and someone had already strung a scrap of old rope to replace the rail she, and Charley, managed to bust in their enthusiasm.

"After you, friend."

Charley laughed and bulled his way through the crowd, clearing a wide enough path for both of them to get to the bar and grab hold of some of the mugs that were being distributed with a frenzied intensity.

"Hardest kickin' opponent I *ever* had," Charley swore happily as he downed the first of what would turn out to be a fair good many beers.

# Chapter 11

It is a funny thing about an investigation. If you go and ask a man about something, and that man happens to know you are an officer of the law, more often than not the SOB will stand there looking you square in the eyes and smile and cheerfully lie to you. Nine times out of ten. Maybe more often than that.

But if you are investigating something *else*—insofar as that same guy knows—he is very likely to tell his lies on the subject he thinks you are investigating and then lead you away from that line of thinking by yammering and yakking about other subjects. Quite often the subjects you really wanted to find out about to begin with.

So there were times, Longarm knew, when a little judicious lying of one's own could pay dividends. This, he figured, just might be one of those times. Avoid getting people's dander up with the mention of race or equality or any of those things that were only gonna make the locals uncomfortable—after all, how comfortable can a man be talking about something when he knows in his gut that he is the one in the wrong—and sneak in through a side door instead.

Hal Denis had said something about his men believing some aging whore was killed by a vigilance committee. Fine. That, then, could be the focus Longarm would admit to here.

But nothing threatening, hmm?

He thought about it while he stood next to his new friend Charley and had another beer.

"So what're you doing here, Longarm?" Charley asked. "Just on a routine sweep through the territory, like?"

Longarm noticed that a number of men standing nearby were paying close attention to the question Charley posed. "Nope, not routine at all," the tall deputy told them. "I'm here on assignment."

"Yeah? An outlaw in Cimarron City? I'll be damn."

"Now Charley, don't you go putting words in my mouth. I said I'm here on an assignment, and I am. I could add that I'm here looking for someone in particular, and that would be true too. But it don't necessarily follow that I'm chasing after an outlaw." Longarm smiled. "Being a deputy ain't always that exciting, you know. There're warrants to serve, summonses, stuff like that. Mostly it's as boring as any other job."

"Yeah?"

"Sure. Take this assignment here, for instance. I'm looking for a woman . . ."

"Ain't we all," someone injected, getting a burst of laughter that was quickly followed by a number of sharp whispers as the freely admitted eavesdroppers called for silence so they could listen in.

"Naw, boys, this is a particular woman I'm looking for. The U.S. attorney up in Denver wants t' talk to her about something. Which I'm not supposed to say anything about but which I can privately tell you ain't half as exciting a proposition as it sounds. Anyway," he said, making it up as he went along, "the boss tells me to come down here and look for her and if she's here take her back up to Denver with me. So that's what I'm doing."

"What about that horse out front? It's sure as shooting a army mount."

" 'Course it is, man. Why would the government pay to hire me a horse at the livery in town here when the same government already owns who the hell knows how many perfectly good horses that're kept right over there at that army post? It's standard procedure for any deputy to borry a horse off the army whenever possible."

"That so?"

"Uh huh. Ask any deputy. It saves tax money."

"Hell, I never knowed the government cared 'bout saving money."

40

Longarm grinned. "With some things they do. Now if it was some congressman that was being asked t' cut back on one o' his privileges, I reckon that might be a different story."

The townspeople of Cimarron City liked that.

"So tell us 'bout this woman you're looking for, Deputy?" a skinny man in sleeve garters asked. He was one of the people Longarm hadn't yet heard a name for.

"Her name is Helen," Longarm said. He paused for a sip of beer. In truth he was frantically trying to remember back to what little Hal Denis had said about the woman who died by hanging here, by her own hand or by foul play depending on whose version you wanted to accept. "Helen Green."

"Helen Green. That don't ring no bells with me," Charley said. "Anybody here know a woman name of Helen Green?"

"Nope." "Not me." "Never heard of such." "I knew a Helen Brown once."

"She might not be using that name here," Longarm added. "For that matter, it might not be her real name at all, just the best one the U.S. attorney could come up with. The woman is a lady of the night, if you understand what I'm saying. And they change names as easy as some folks change underwear."

"Oftener than Mike there changes his, I bet," someone said, prompting laughter and more interest among the men standing close by.

"We got us a whole bunch o' whores in town, Long," a man whose name was Randy offered. "White whores, nigger whores, Indian whores, we even got us a couple chink whores over at Fat Kate's."

"Just think, boys," another voice injected. "Deppity Long here is gonna get paid by our gov'mint to visit all the whorehouses in Cimarron City."

"D'you get paid to screw 'em too, Longarm?"

"Just talk to 'em. Dang it." He grinned.

"I think I done went into the wrong line of work. I shoulda growed up and been a deputy marshal."

"Yeah, and your wife would snatch you bald-headed if ever you set foot in any one of them places, Bert."

"Hell, she'd have to let me if it was my job."

"So how are you gonna find this Helen Green, Longarm?"

He shrugged. "I have a description. It isn't much account, but it'll have to do. An older woman. For a whore, anyhow. Not much to look at so she probably goes cheap. Crib girl, more'n likely. Too old and faded to be particular. She has the reputation of taking on anything with the price of admission."

"But what's she look like, Longarm? Fat, thin, what?"

"If the U.S. attorney or anybody in his office knows, they didn't let on to my boss or to me, boys. What I've told you is everything I know." He grinned again. "Sure ain't much, is it?"

"It sure ain't."

"Is there a reward for finding this here Helen Green?" a man who was several days in need of a shave asked.

"Sorry. No reward for her. I told you the case they want to question her about isn't all that exciting."

"Damn. I could use me some easy money."

"Couldn't we all."

"Hey! Bernie! We're getting awful dry over here. Keep them beers coming."

"Long as Charley an' Deputy Long are paying for 'em anyhow."

The mood of the men in the place was good, Longarm saw.

And now there wasn't a man in Cimarron City who should be feeling threatened by the presence of Custis Long.

"Care for one of these cheroots, friend Charley?"

"Thankee, Longarm. Here, have another beer."

Longarm snapped a lucifer afire and held the flame for both of them to get their cheroots started, then accepted the beer Charley had captured for him from among those that were being slid down the length of the once polished but now rather soggy bar top.

"Damn, Longarm, I'm sure glad I didn't come to stomp your face in out there," Charley said happily.

"Then I'd say we're both glad—that I didn't stomp you."

Charley roared and slapped Longarm across the back.

The evening, Longarm thought, was gonna turn out to be just about as soggy as that bar top was getting. He smiled and let things take their own course for the time being.

# Chapter 12

Longarm wasn't drunk. He had too much capacity to hold his liquor than to let himself get loopy on a few lousy beers. Or even on a great many lousy beers.

But if he'd been pressed on the subject he would've had to admit to being just the least little bit, well, soggy. Somewhere underneath the roots of his hair.

The best thing, he figured, would be to get back to Camp Good Enough and see if he could promote some quarters courtesy of the government that employed him and the infantry boys out there.

Charley was still inside the saloon and still going strong. Longarm had no idea when Charley figured this free-beer largess of theirs was supposed to come to a stop, but apparently that time hadn't been reached yet.

Whoever owned the saloon was likely having an all-time record night of it because the freely flowing beer not only brought customers in to keep the place packed to capacity, it rendered their judgment faulty and was leading to some rip-roaring play at the faro and poker tables.

All in all, one helluva night in Cimarron City, Longarm reflected as he took a second stab at the stirrup of his McClellan. Somehow he'd missed it the first try.

He belched and gathered his reins, swung the bay out into the street and let it pick its way back in the direction of Good Enough.

Good enough for what, he wondered. He'd have to remember to ask somebody.

Damn bay they'd given him sure was one slow and wobbly son of a bitch. He was gonna have to fuss at somebody. Make sure he got a decent horse next time. Why, this one was so hard a ride that it was making his stomach queasy.

Damn thing was somehow making his forehead hot, too, and turning his cheeks numb.

Stupid damn horse.

Stupid damn country around here, too.

Ghosts in this country, by damn.

He could see 'em. Kinda catch glimpses out of the corners of his eyes, like.

There was never anything there when he looked straight on to try and get a good look at them.

Cheeky, sneaky damn ghosts.

But whenever he looked straight ahead along the trail to Good Enough he could glimpse the figures and the movement off to the side there.

Cheeky sons o' bitches.

Trying to hurry him along, weren't they. Well, he'd show 'em. He'd take his own sweet time, and the hell with the ghosts.

Piss on a bunch o' ghosts.

That seemed such a good idea that he hauled the bay to a stop, got down and took a piss.

That felt better.

He upchucked too. Just a little bit. And that felt the best of all.

Feeling considerably better then, he stepped back up onto the bay and put it into a lope for Good Enough.

This time he didn't see any ghost figures in the shadows alongside the trail.

# Chapter 13

Longarm felt . . . shitty. Bloated and brittle and jumpy. His head ached and there was a vile taste in his mouth. Except for those things, though, he was none the worse for wear. Or so he would have liked to convince himself.

"Good morning, SIR!" The soldier snapped to rigid attention with a sharp click of his heels and a loud slap of flesh against wood when he executed a rifle salute. Longarm winced. "With the commander's compliments, sir, Cap'n Denis invites you to join him in the officers' mess. SIR!"

Longarm winced again. "That'd be my pleasure, young man."

"Thank you, sir. Do you know the way, sir?"

He'd been shown the way yesterday. But that had been an awful long time ago. Besides, this morning it would be a fair trick if he could find his butt when he needed to wipe. He allowed as how he wasn't entirely sure about that.

"At your convenience, sir, I will wait and take you to join the gen'l'men." A faint hint of soft, sibilant drawl right at the end there was the only trace of accent in the midnight black soldier's voice.

"Very good, Private. I won't be long." Longarm rubbed a hand over his beard stubble and stifled a groan. Hell, getting a move on was what he needed anyhow. He bit back a yawn and went about getting the day started.

"Good morning, Hal. Gentlemen." He nodded a greeting to the three junior officers who were already at the table and accepted the introductions performed by Capt. Denis. There was a first lieutenant named Wyche who was commander of one of the line companies, a second lieutenant named Felix—Longarm wasn't sure if that was the guy's first name or last—who was commander of the headquarters company and post quartermaster, and another second lieutenant named Grable whose duties weren't specified in the course of the introduction. And who probably wouldn't be capable of explaining them if Longarm asked him.

All the junior officers were cut from poor cloth. As a group they were misfits . . . alcoholics or liars or incompetents or worse. But Grable seemed in a class by himself. He acted like he was more than mildly addled. Whether that was an accident of birth or a more recent development brought on by drink or drugs or maybe the debilitating stages of syphilis Longarm couldn't guess. For whatever reason the poor SOB was a glassy-eyed drooler who needed assistance to feed himself. An unfair example of the sort of officer who was deemed good enough to command colored troops, Longarm hoped.

Longarm smiled and nodded. And took a seat at the long table as far from Grable as he could manage.

"So. Custis." Hal Denis was depressingly cheery and bright this morning. "How may we help you today?"

By keepin' your voice down. That was what Longarm wanted to tell the man. He didn't. He played the role of the respectful guest and didn't try to snap at his host or throw things. "Can't think of a single thing more, Hal. I'm doing fine, thanks." Why, he even managed to smile.

"Anything you need, you know. Anything at all," Denis persisted.

"Thank you, Hal."

"Coffee, suh?" The waiter at his elbow looked like he'd been carved out of oiled mahogany. The soldier wore a crisply starched white jacket and carried an ornate serving pot of heavy silver. Only some conditions at Camp Good Enough fell into the category of roughing it.

"Son, I think you may've just saved my life." Longarm gulped down that first reviving cup and gestured for a refill. After that he was willing—and marginally able—to face the thought of actual food.

• • •

Longarm had no idea who had taken care of the bay horse last night. He knew he hadn't done it. Fortunately somebody had. The horse was delivered to him with its coat brushed until it fairly gleamed, and with Longarm's saddle and bridle freshly cleaned and oiled as well. Maybe there was something to be said about this idea of having subordinates around to tend to the details.

"Thank you, soldier."

"Any time, suh." The man popped to attention and saluted, which Longarm's civilian capacity didn't warrant. Longarm mentioned that to him but the private first class only grinned and said, "I already know that, suh."

Longarm accepted the bay's reins and swung onto the saddle. He was feeling better now that he'd managed to surround some breakfast. He felt damn near human. He turned away from the sagging tent that served as visiting officers' quarters here and headed back toward Cimarron City.

# Chapter 14

One good purpose was served the night before, Longarm noticed as he rode into town. The people he saw on the street were friendly now. There was none of the suspicion that frequently greets the arrival of a stranger. Now the people of Cimarron City knew him, knew why he was here— well, thought they did—and knew—or anyway believed— he was no threat to them.

That was certainly a leg up from the usual order of things.

Once again he tied the bay to a hitch ring, this time in front of a general mercantile, and ambled indoors.

"Good morning, Longarm."

"Good morning. Um, Drew isn't it?"

The man looked pleased. He grinned. "You have a good memory."

"Not good enough to remember which mule it was that kicked me when I wasn't looking last night."

"Here." The storekeeper fetched a blue-and-white package of headache powders down off his shelving and took out an envelope. He uncorked a soda bottle and poured the powder into it. The mixture foamed and bubbled in a most unappetizing manner. Longarm was reluctant to drink anything that acted like it was working up to exploding, but he couldn't hardly refuse now that Drew had gone and made the concoction.

"Bottoms up." The stuff was gritty going down but didn't actually taste that bad. And it sat in his stomach better than he'd expected too. This morning's breakfast and last night's excesses hadn't been getting along all that well during the ride in from Good Enough.

"Better?" Drew asked.

Longarm belched. Then again. The gases coming out of his belly tasted nasty, but he sure felt better once they were gone. "Yeah. Yeah, I think maybe so." He smiled. "What do I owe you, Drew?"

"Owe me? Hell, Longarm, you don't owe me nothing." The storekeeper grinned. "Much beer as you bought for me last night, I reckon I can set you up to one little powder and a sody pop in exchange of it."

"Bought you that much did I?"

"Wait till you see the bill."

"Really?"

"Your pal Charley Hamer," Drew chuckled, "something you really ought to know, Longarm . . . that Charley is one awful nice fella. Heart as big as all outdoors. Always wanting to treat his friends to anything they want. But, uh . . . how do I tell you this?"

"Spit it out, Drew."

"Yeah, well, the thing is . . . Charley has the best intentions in the world, Longarm. You got to understand that. And he'll pull his own weight. I mean, he honest t' Pete intends to. You know what I'm saying?"

"Intends to," Longarm repeated, mouthing the words like they didn't taste real good.

"Uh huh."

"What you're saying, Drew, is that Charley wasn't lying to me."

"Oh no, he'd never do that to a friend."

"But Charley might be just a lee-tle bit short when it comes time for us t' divvy up the bar tab the two of us run up last night?"

"A little short. Now that surely is a nice way to put it, Longarm."

"In this case a little bit amounting to, um, all of it?"

"Approximately," Drew agreed.

Longarm shuddered. And gulped down the remainder of the soda pop and headache powder. He'd have quaffed a double shot of rye whiskey if he'd had one handy. Or a bowl of hemlock, which might really have been the best idea. But at the moment the fizzy soda was the best he could do.

"You feeling all right, Longarm?" Drew asked solicitously. "You don't look so good again."

# Chapter 15

Longarm strode in the direction of the saloon that he remembered all too well from last night. There was no point in putting this off any longer.

"Señor?"

"Yes?" He stopped where he was in the middle of the street and swept his hat off. He smiled. It would have been rude to rush off. "Yes, señorita?" The girl was pretty. Pretty? Hell, she was gorgeous. Probably not yet twenty. Heart-shaped face. Lush figure. Lips full and moist and just made to be kissed. Black hair hanging loose and falling all the way to the small of her back. Low-cut peasant blouse that emphasized the depth of the valley between her mountains. Uh, breasts. Tiny ankles. Slender, delicate neck. Eyes dark and wet and big enough to swim in. Sharply chiseled nose with a tiny dent or crease right on the tip of it. Ears pierced, with silver hoops dangling from them, each hoop just about big enough to enclose a whiskey keg. All right, a small whiskey keg then. Cheek bones high and prominent enough to think there might be some Indio branches on the old family tree but skin coloring so creamy pale a satin that it seemed pretty sure there were Castilians in the background too. Impossibly small waist. Altogether . . . Longarm realized he was taking so long admiring her that the look had become a stare and at this point he was being rude. He cleared his throat and forced himself to look away from those huge, moist, beautiful eyes. "Yes, miss?"

She smiled and came to a stop in front of him. "You are the Señor Long, yes?"

"I am Deputy Long. Yes," he agreed.

"My master wishes to invite you . . ."

"Master?" he said with a quick frown.

The girl became flustered. Which hadn't been his intention at all. It was just that the word seemed so strange. . . .

"Is this how to say? Master, no?"

"No, not master. Employer," he corrected.

"Thank you, Señor Long. My employ wishes you to be his guest at the luncheon today."

"And your employ*er* is . . . ?"

"My master . . . I mean my . . . my . . ."

"Sorry. No, I mean it. Please go on. Pretend I never said anything 'bout that."

"Thank you." She smiled. When she smiled it was kinda like another sun was turned on. Except this new one was brighter than the old one ever thought of being. "My master is the Señor Sherman, señor. Up there?" She pointed toward the bluff that commanded the valley of Big Skull Wash and at the magnificent house that commanded the bluff. "My master is that señor, señor." She smiled again. My oh my but it was something when she did that, Longarm reflected.

"You say there is a luncheon?"

"Si, señor. In your honor to make your acquaintance, señor."

"Today?"

"Sí, señor."

Longarm pulled his Ingersol out and glanced at the time. It was far short of noon.

"I will tell him you come, yes?"

Why not, Longarm thought. Before long he'd have to start making his rounds of the whorehouses. He was gonna have to do that until somebody helped out by informing him that the woman the people here thought he was looking for was actually dead and buried. Then, of course, he could start raising questions about how she died and get into the matter of whether there was or wasn't a committee of vigilance operating in Cimarron City.

But, shit, he couldn't start knocking on whorehouse doors at this time of day. The ladies wouldn't be stirring for hours yet, and the houses wouldn't open for business until the middle of the afternoon or later.

53

There wasn't any reason why he shouldn't go up atop the bluff and meet this Colonel Sherman. Who, he'd been told, never hobnobbed with anybody from Cimarron City or from Camp Good Enough.

Curious, that. Longarm suspected he'd have been willing to go even if he didn't want an excuse to see this marvelously beautiful young girl again.

"Please inform Señor Sherman, Colonel Sherman that is, that I would be honored to join him for luncheon today." He made an elegant bow to the lass and winked at her.

The girl giggled and whirled, skipping away with a dancer's lithe grace and breaking into a run. "I will tell my master."

"Wait! What's your name?"

But the girl either did not hear or chose not to respond. She disappeared into an alley and was lost from view.

Longarm blinked and shook his head. Damn.

But he expected he was in for it now. A luncheon with the master of the manor, eh? He chuckled and resumed his walk toward the saloon, wondering just how much this bar tab was gonna turn out to be. But in truth distracted by recurring thoughts of that fantastically exciting girl. Lucky son of a bitch this colonel to have so beautiful a señorita call him master.

# Chapter 16

Luncheon. The time hadn't ever been specified. And now
the girl had disappeared. There wasn't anyone else handy
he could get his answers from. And not only on the subject
of what time a guest might be expected for lunch. Longarm
asked several townspeople about Sherman, but the people
of Cimarron City knew, or admitted to knowing, damn
little more than Vickery had already said. No one in town
seemed actually to have met the man and few had so much
as glimpsed him.

First name? Colonel was all anyone Longarm spoke with
had ever heard. Colonel Sherman. No other names or initials
given. Everyone had heard that he was supposed to be kin to
the justly famous General William Tecumseh Sherman. But
no one knew just exactly what the relationship was supposed
to be. The speculation ran from illegitimate half-brother to
third cousin once removed. Whatever the hell a third cousin
once removed was supposed to be.

The folks knew for sure that their neighbor ran some
cows. They knew that because he employed a few cowhands
who came down off the bluff now and then to have their
ashes hauled and to sop up some liquor. The good and
gossipy folks of Cimarron City were also pretty sure that
raising cows wasn't what the colonel did for his livelihood because the hands—who must have been coached
to say nothing because in fact they said little—talked like
the herds weren't very large and weren't very difficult to
handle.

Except for that? Damned little. Wherever the household
shopping was done, it wasn't down here in Cimarron City.

Wherever the house staff went to spend their money, and their free time, it wasn't here. If workmen or extra help were ever needed on top of the bluff, the hiring wasn't done down here.

The folks of Cimarron City felt snubbed.

Also almighty curious.

There isn't much of anything calculated to raise more in the way of speculation or of awe than a cold and deliberate lack of knowledge. That Longarm knew.

Of wild rumor he had aplenty to sift through. Of substance rather less.

The house was inhabited, for sure, by the colonel and his lady and an elderly gentleman. Also by a staff of unknown size and duties. At least two different Mexican females had been seen, presumably including the girl who'd come down this morning to find Deputy Long. Aside from that . . . *nada*. Or mighty close to *nada*.

Before the morning was over and Longarm could reasonably start out for his luncheon with the best available local substitute for royalty, he had listened to several score outlandish tales that purported to explain all about the colonel, the colonel's lady, and the grandiose manor house that sneered down at the less fortunate dwellers in the valley of the Big Skull.

The colonel, he was told, was a refugee from one of the many revolutions in Mexico; in that role the colonel was said to have absconded with a fortune that he had been asked to guard on behalf of his *jefe*.

The colonel, Longarm was told, was a cripple, his body shattered in a gallant charge at Gettysburg. No, at Vicksburg. No, he was wounded while repelling a charge at The Wilderness. Physically the colonel was fine, but his nerve had been shattered and now his brother William Tecumseh saw to all his material needs but could not abide having the colonel close where his debilities would be on view of the public. That informant also reminded Longarm that the general would soon be running for the office of the presidency and as president would soon enough be Longarm's boss. Longarm considered himself suitably warned on that score. Sure he did.

The colonel, Longarm was told, had a dark past. And a mistress who lived with the colonel and the colonel's lady in the big house on the bluff.

The colonel's lady, Longarm was told, was the recluse in the family, not the colonel at all. The lady had degenerated into lunacy, the result of a disorder persistent in her family. She was an unfortunate embarrassment and the reason there could be no children. The colonel's love for her was such that he preferred to hide himself away, too, rather than be parted from her as he would have to be in more civilized surroundings.

The colonel, Longarm was informed in the strictest confidence, was the black sheep of the Sherman family and fought on the side of the Confederacy during the past unpleasantness. That, the whispering informant explained, was why Colonel Sherman now was in an enforced exile here on the plains. If he attempted to leave and return to society to claim his place as head of the powerful Sherman family, he would be murdered. In fact, that was why the army post had been established here, to spy on Colonel Sherman and to assassinate him if he attempted to leave the immediate vicinity of the house General Sherman had had built for him.

Most of these stories, it should be understood, were offered free of charge. But with a request that the deputy be kind enough to repeat his generosity of the night before. Or repeat at the least that portion of the generosity which applied to the informant who was now so eager to assist Longarm in any possible way, including giving him all the information they had on the colonel who lived in the big house inside of which no one in Cimarron City had ever actually been.

In each case Longarm gladly—if with a grain of salt or several—accepted the tale but not the sponsorship of another drinking bout. After all, the bar tab he'd already cleared by way of a government travel voucher was big enough to clean out the bulk of his entire life savings—well, he wasn't known for his devotion to thrift and wise investment, after all—if the damn pencil pushers rejected the expenditure. If, and when, a showdown with the auditors came he didn't want to compound his troubles by adding onto the amount.

So he listened, and laughed quite a lot at the preposterous notions these folks came up with, and as soon as he reasonably could he went to see for himself what the colonel was like.

Custis Long didn't consider it particularly amazing to discover that no one in Cimarron City had come even close to telling him what the colonel was like.

# Chapter 17

"Marshal Long, I believe. Welcome to our home, Marshal, and please do come in. I am Victoria Sherman."

Longarm removed his hat and made a leg toward the girl. "Your father is in I presume, Miss Sherman?"

She tipped her head back and laughed. "Had I known I would be so outrageously complimented, sir, I should have insisted upon a stream of invitations months and months ago. Come in, please, and I shall tell my husband you are here. If I dare. If you flatter him that shamelessly, sir, I shall be forced to live with a swollen headed old poop for many months to come." She stepped back from the door and motioned for Longarm to enter. The Mexican girl who'd been in town earlier materialized at his elbow now to take his hat. Another girl almost as pretty had met him out front to take the bay and lead it away.

But pretty as the hired help were, there was something about Victoria Sherman. . . .

Longarm hadn't been flattering her. He'd genuinely thought that Mrs. Sherman must surely be the colonel's daughter. She seemed scarcely old enough to be any man's wife. And the wife of a retired officer? Incredible.

Seventeen? he guessed. Eighteen at the outside. She still had the brisk, energetic step of vigorous youth, and her skin had the healthy glow of it shining through from within.

It was her energy, Longarm realized once he thought about it, that kept the girl—he couldn't bring himself to think of her as a woman, never mind her marital state—from being plain. Certainly there was nothing exceptional in her features. She was small, almost tiny, the top of her head not quite reaching Longarm's shoulders. She had hair of a very ordinary brown shade and eyes so shyly lowered that he never saw enough of them to judge what color they might have been. Her hair was drawn back in what should have seemed a quite matronly bun. Yet there was such a rich and gleaming liveliness in the way it caught the light that it wasn't plain at all. Her dress was a confused confection of brocade and lace and tassels. Most gowns done in that particular style made Longarm think of lampshades. But not this one. Victoria Sherman's bearing and carriage were so pert and lively that even a dress as dull and stodgy as that was made to appear youthful and attractive.

As for her features they were . . . plain. Ordinary. Almost bland. Yet in combination the whole exceeded the parts to somehow become quietly attractive. Her face was thin, her mouth small, and her lips pale. Her cheeks were hollowed and her neck so slender it seemed hardly possible that it could support her head. Yet there was something about her, some inner quality that glowed through from within . . . Longarm could not hope to name it. He could only recognize it when he saw it. And applaud it on those exceptionally rare occasions when, as now, that occurred.

Victoria Sherman disappeared in one direction and the Mexican girl in another, and Longarm was left alone in the foyer that occupied the central part of the tall house. He stood, not sure what to do with his hands, and looked about.

Grand as it was from the outside, the inside of the place was common enough. Not common exactly but certainly not the expression of great wealth Longarm's conversations in town had led him to expect. The house was more large than it was rich.

The floors were of holystoned wooden planking. Nothing extravagant like parquet or imported tile. The furnishings were nice but ordinary, the sort of sturdy and utilitarian things that could be found in any hotel lobby catering to a good but not wealthy class of commercial traveler. The wallpaper was the same cheap stuff that could be found in almost any general store, and the draperies were made of a decent and durable fabric that was no more exclusive than the wallpaper.

Longarm obviously couldn't judge the layout of the entire house by the little piece of it he could see from the foyer, but the downstairs appeared to consist of a parlor and dining room to one side of the foyer and a library and possibly an office on the other side. He guessed there would be a kitchen at the back. Victoria Sherman had gone to the left, toward the room he suspected was an office, while the Mexican girl, whose name he still didn't know, went down a short hall toward where a kitchen ought to be.

All in all Longarm would've had to say that the Sherman mansion wasn't all that special a hacienda. Nice enough but certainly not elegant.

And the colonel? Longarm hid a smile. Hell, after seeing Mrs. Sherman he was willing to believe that colonel was the guy's first name not his title and that he was twenty years old and was working here as manager for somebody else. Like maybe some well-heeled British investment company getting into the cow business and wanting a big house to entertain stockholders in when they were touring on this side of the Atlantic.

That story right there made more sense than most of those he'd heard down in town earlier.

Then he heard footsteps slowly approaching and knew that he could finally quit guessing. Longarm checked to see that his collar ends weren't sticking up and that his fly was buttoned. Once those were done he figured he was ready for anybody or anything that might come through that door.

Ready, that is, until he saw the man who did appear in the doorway.

The fellow was . . . ancient. Had to be in his seventies at the very least. Maybe his eighties.

He was small and shriveled, bent over with the rheumatism and barely able to get along even with the assistance of a cane held in each gnarled hand.

The man's neck was so wattled and loose he looked like a turkey gobbler, and there were liver spots on his hands and one cheek.

Copper and yellow discolorations on the front of his trousers showed that he was given to dribbling on himself when he peed, and the poor old fellow trembled and shook

61

when he moved. Victoria had to help him along with a supporting hand beneath his elbow lest he lose his balance and topple over sideways.

The thought of this decrepit old fart snuggled up in bed with a young and innocent girl like Victoria, the thought of him warming himself between her thighs, of those twisted hands groping and fondling and pushing inside her taut and tender flesh, of that gap-toothed mouth slobbering all over her . . .

Shit, Longarm grumbled.

Not that he had any right to think such a thing . . . not that he had any right to think anything at all, but . . . well . . . shit.

Longarm smiled and strode forward with his hand extended for the old fart to shake. "It's a pleasure to finally meet you, Colonel. And thank you for inviting me here today, sir."

# Chapter 18

Victoria Sherman threw her head back and this time she didn't just laugh, she roared. "Marshal Long, you outdo yourself."

"Ma'am?"

She grinned up at him. "Marshal Long, I should like you to meet my father, Angus MacKay. Da, this is the gentleman I was telling you about." She guided the old fellow into the parlor and toward a chair, her voice floating back over her shoulder to Longarm who was standing in the foyer with egg on his face. "My husband will be down shortly, Marshal. Won't you join us in a drink while we wait?"

The wait was interminably long. Or maybe it only seemed that way. Longarm sat there with a glass of untasted red wine in his hand, listening to Victoria and her dad make small talk and pretend that there wasn't a first-class idiot sitting in the room with them. But they were nice about it. Neither of them actually *said* any of the things they must surely be thinking.

Longarm gathered that MacKay was fairly recently retired from some unspecified profession, the sort of thing anyway that utilizes a man's mind and talents rather than his muscle as the basis for his livelihood. Also that the onset of physical difficulties—those that had been obvious when Longarm first saw him—forced the retirement. Apparently Victoria's father wasn't as old as he looked. Longarm concentrated on sitting still and keeping his big mouth closed for a change.

When Col. Willard T. Sherman finally made his appearance, he turned out to be a handsome man of middle years, call it mid- to late forties or thereabouts, with touches of distinguished gray at his temples. He had dark hair and a pencil mustache, was about five-feet-ten and of slight build. He wore a dark gray suit with matching vest, highly polished opera shoes, and a tie so neatly knotted he must have just finished forming it.

"Welcome. Welcome to The Folly," he greeted, shaking Longarm's hand and smiling warmly. Longarm found himself responding to the gentleman's infectious charm. For the first time in some little while he was able to smile too.

"Thank you, Colonel. But . . . The Folly?"

Sherman laughed. "Acquiescence to the inevitable, Marshal. Everyone says I'm foolish to have built to such a scale so far from what passes for civilization in our society. It is a subject that I have my own views about, of course. But I am perfectly well aware of the things that are said about my, shall we say, unusual business decision here." The man smiled again. He seemed an awfully nice fellow, Longarm thought.

"At least you recognize that it's unusual," Longarm observed.

"Certainly," Sherman agreed, fussing with the bowl of his pipe while he settled himself into a massive armchair before the now cold fireplace. "But then great victories are not won by the faint heart nor the small measure. Vision and commitment, Marshal, those are the qualities needed for great success. And my dear family and I shall succeed here, sir. Greatly so, if I have my way about it."

"I wish you no less than everything you're working for," Longarm said, toasting the gentleman with the wine glass he'd been handed earlier. He discovered that he was meaning every word of it too. Victoria's husband seemed quite the fellow.

"Thank you, Long. Thank you. That is decent of you." He smiled and leaned forward as if to rise. "Refill on that? . . . Ah, my dear man, you are not a wine fancier, I see. What would be more to your taste, eh? Bourbon? Or perhaps some of my dear father-in-law's Scots whiskey? I stock it by the case for him, you know." He said that last part pleasantly enough. But Longarm could see that there was a kernel of maliciousness hidden inside the casual words and the charming smile. A tiff between Sherman and Victoria's father? Apparently. The interesting thing so far as Longarm was concerned was to see that there were sharp claws hidden within the velvet paws of Willard Sherman.

Longarm pretended not to notice. "You wouldn't have any rye on hand, would you?"

"I have what I am told is the finest rye ever distilled. Perhaps I could solicit your opinion about that, Marshal? It would be a great favor to me as I don't care for the flavor of spirits myself and have been trusting to the judgment of the supplier. One must always be chary of that, mm?"

"Reckon I'd be willing to help a man out," Longarm said with a wink and a grin.

Instead of getting up and going over to the cabinet where the wines were kept, Sherman sank back in his chair with a glance toward an unobtrusive door set into the back wall. Within seconds the door opened, and one of the Mexican girls came out to curtsy to her master. Sherman issued orders in Spanish that were much too slurred and rapid for Longarm to catch even a hint of meaning. The girl curtsied again and trotted over to the liquor cabinet to fetch a glass and bottle. She brought them to Longarm and poured only a small splash of liquor into the glass, standing by with the bottle to see if he approved before she served any more of it.

Longarm tasted of it.

"Well?" Sherman asked.

"It's rye, all right," Longarm conceded.

"But is it the best rye you've ever had?" the gentleman insisted.

"I . . . you want the truth, don't you?"

"Indeed I do, sir. I ask for no less than the complete truth here."

"Colonel, I can say in all honesty that this here stuff is rye whiskey."

"But . . . ?"

"But it ain't what you'd call very good rye whiskey. 'Bout average. Maybe a mite less'n that. It'd make a good bar whiskey."

Col. Willard T. Sherman flushed a dark and mottled shade of purple. Victoria rose partway out of her chair, but he motioned her back.

"Colonel, I never meant . . ."

"No. You did not. Of course you did not." For some reason Sherman sent a venomous look toward his father-in-law, who was studiously pretending to be unaware of any of this. "Please," the colonel said. "My apologies. Now is not the time . . . not at all." He regained control of himself, visibly shuddered once and then said something more in that double-quick Spanish. The Mexican girl curtsied once again and plucked the offending whiskey glass out of Longarm's fingers. She took the glass and bottle with her and left the room.

If anybody'd asked, Longarm would've admitted to being more than a trifle disappointed. After all, ordinary rye whiskey is a helluva lot better than no rye whiskey. But apparently that wasn't a choice he was gonna be given. Apparently the odd colonel here wanted things done to the nines or not at all. Except if that was so, why did he settle for less than the best when it came to his furnishings and draperies and stuff? Didn't he know better? Maybe not. Good thing that wasn't something Longarm had to figure out.

Longarm had been distracted for a moment there. Now he realized that everybody else was getting up. Sherman hadn't said anything but there must've been some sort of signal given. The colonel, his lady, and the lady's father were rising and standing there giving Longarm expectant looks.

"We shall go in now, Marshal," Victoria said graciously. She came to his side and placed a tiny hand on the crook of his elbow, allowing the guest to "lead" her into the dining room although in truth it was she who subtly directed the way. Her father was left to totter along with his canes, and her husband brought up the rear of this small procession.

The dining table was long enough to seat fourteen, half a dozen on each side and one at each end. Places were formally laid at the two ends and again to the right of each end chair. Longarm was directed to sit at the colonel's right. Angus MacKay was placed to the right of his daughter. There was so much bare, polished wood between the two ends of the table that it would have been impossible for the diners to pass a salt cellar or a platter without rising and going for a short walk. Not that that was apt to be necessary. Both Mexican girls were on hand to see to the needs of the participants in the luncheon.

The meal consisted of a young and tender prairie chicken served whole on each plate, much like squab or game hen might have been in city surroundings. There were also canned vegetables and fresh rolls. The table linen was actually cotton, Longarm noticed, and the silver wasn't even plated but was polished steel. The elegance of the table, he saw, was a pretense.

Colonel Sherman, he guessed, was striving for real wealth, hence his venture here in the middle of nowhere, and in the meantime intended to comport himself as if he were already wealthy.

And if the man didn't realize that wealth and true elegance are not synonymous, that in fact they are not even related, well, that too was the colonel's business and nothing to do with Custis Long. Thank goodness.

Longarm smiled and nodded and chewed his way through the meal while Victoria and MacKay sat in silence at the far end of the table, and at the nearer end Sherman rambled about calving percentages and feed/gain ratios and other stuff that Longarm didn't even try to understand. It all sounded as dry as if it'd come out of a textbook, but the cook damn sure knew how to roast a prairie chicken so it came out juicy and tender enough to fall off the bone. Knew how to stir up a bread dough, too, and so was close to Longarm's heart right there t' begin with.

The meal didn't take very long since the only one doing any talking was the host, and he didn't eat much. When everybody was finished, Victoria took her father and led him away, saying something about it being time for the old gentleman's nap. Once she was gone the brandy and cigars were presented, the cigars to both men and the brandy only to Longarm. But then Sherman had said something about being a teetotaler. Longarm could get along without brandy himself and never miss it, but Willard Sherman's taste in cigars was as good as his taste in rye whiskey was poor. It'd been a power of time since Longarm had tasted the equal of one of the fat, pale things that came out of Sherman's humidor. He even enjoyed the process of getting it lighted. The pretty Mexican girl who'd been in town earlier handled the chore for him, delicately doing all the nipping and trimming, bathing the wrapper leaf in a silver dish of brandy and then warming the damp cigar carefully over a diffused candle flame before she lighted it by way of another candle and finally presented it to Longarm. It was the sort of hoity-toity process that is pretentious and silly only when it's being done for the other guy. When it is done for oneself it comes across as a right pleasant idea. Longarm gave in and let himself enjoy it.

Eventually the girls withdrew from the dining room, leaving Longarm and the colonel alone at the big table.

"Victoria and I seldom invite guests to our home," Sherman said.

"I'd heard that, Colonel."

"Had you? Then perhaps you appreciate that I had a motive beyond the pleasure of your company, pleasant though that has been, when I chose to ask you here."

"Do tell."

Sherman smiled, then expanded the smile into laughter. "Don't go all rustic and boyish on me now, Longarm."

The tall deputy raised an eyebrow. The nickname hadn't been mentioned in this house before. Not by him it hadn't, anyway.

"Yes, I've heard of you. Long before you arrived in Cimarron City, in fact. Your reputation precedes you, sir. A most enviable reputation it is too."

"Thanks. I guess."

"The reason I wanted to meet you, Longarm . . . may I call you that? Thank you," he rolled on without actually pausing. "The reason I wanted to meet you, Longarm, is that I have a vested interest in the well-being of this entire district. After all, I have committed myself to this land. I want it to remain an agreeable locale. So naturally I intend to do everything in my power to see that law and order is maintained here."

"Of course, Colonel." There was, Longarm noticed, no suggestion that the colonel be called Willard, even though

68

Willard felt free to call the deputy by a nickname.

"I happen to know that your presence here has nothing to do with any prostitute named Helen Green."

"Oh, really?" Longarm sat up a bit straighter in his chair. His eyes narrowed a fraction of an inch, and all of a sudden the colonel's cigar didn't taste quite as good as it had a moment earlier.

"You are here because of the frictions between the colored troops at Camp Good Enough and those short-sighted fools down in the town."

Longarm gritted his teeth and damn near bit through the end of that excellent cigar.

"Calm down, Longarm. I can see that you are not delighted to hear that I am privy to your secret. Well, sir, you have naught to fear from me. I want only to assist you in any way possible. I mean that, sir. In *any* way possible. If you need information, my sources may be broader ranging than you suspect. If you need money to bribe informants, you have only to ask. In defense of my own admittedly selfish interests, Longarm, I want to assist your investigation in every way possible."

"Really?"

Sherman nodded. "It is well known within the military leadership, Longarm, that I have rather firm opinions about the situation here. In fact, it was I who precipitated your assignment here by way of my repeated complaints to those idiots at Fort Lyons."

"Oh?"

"They were unwise to put Good Enough here to begin with, Longarm. I told them so at the time. In fact, I have petitioned certain friends of mine in Washington City for the removal of the post from this location. It should be removed to the north of the Arkansas River if it is to be effective as a police agency along the national cattle droving road. Or relocated several days ride to the east if it is to play any role in policing the unassigned lands of the Indian Territories. Or rebuilt someplace where there is adequate water and graze if the army wants a Remount station. As it is, you see, the post has three duties and is capable of performing none of them. I've been telling my friends in Washington City all along that the role of this station must be adequately defined and the post moved to a place that will facilitate the successful completion of those duties. But this present situation must not be allowed to continue."

"That's a right interesting theory, Colonel."

"In the meantime, of course, until the camp is relocated, I want a harmonious situation around me. So I repeat my statement, Longarm. I stand willing and able to assist you in any way you might require."

"One thing I can think of right off the top o' my head, Colonel."

"Name it, sir, and if it is within my power I promise it shall be yours."

"I've heard rumor that there's a committee o' vigilance operating in Cimarron City. You heard anything about that?"

"I have heard the same rumors. In fact, I have heard it presented as more than rumor. I understand there is indeed such a group of night-riding cowards in existence there."

"You got any hard information, Colonel? Who's involved, for instance? An' are they the ones that hanged that woman?"

"I have no names. But it is clearly my understanding that they did in fact commit the murder and then engineered the false ruling of suicide in an effort to protect themselves."

Longarm grunted. Sherman wasn't just parroting back Longarm's own words. The man obviously was familiar with the matter of the dead whore.

"If you want to know more, Longarm, I shall direct my sources to find out. As quickly as possible, sir. When I learn more I shall pass the information along immediately."

"That's awful kind o' you, Colonel."

"I offered to help. I meant it."

"An' I do appreciate it." Longarm stood. "Reckon I've taken up more of your time than I really ought, Colonel. If I can give Miz Sherman my respects now, sir, I'll be on my way."

"Mrs. Sherman will be nursing our daughter at this time of day, Longarm."

"Sir?" Longarm blurted.

"We have a babe yet in arms. Didn't you know?"

"Uh, no."

"Oh, yes. Almost six months old now. She should be getting teeth soon. I presume Victoria will consent to put her on bottle feedings then. For now, though, Victoria must interrupt her schedule at least four times daily for the convenience of the child."

"Yes, well, uh . . . yes." Longarm coughed into his fist. Lordy! It wasn't just every man who was so open as to talk about his wife having a babe sucking at her tit.

"Perhaps it would be best if I convey your respects and your thanks to Mrs. Sherman, Longarm."

"Yes, sir, I do think that might be for the best. Thank you."

"Of course." The colonel led Longarm out through the foyer and to the front door, where one of the Mexican girls was waiting with his Stetson already in hand. "Thank you, Carlotta." Sherman took the hat from the girl and transferred it into Longarm's hands. "I shall inform you as quickly as I learn anything more, Longarm. Count on it."

"Thank you, Colonel. For everything."

Sherman smiled and trailed him out onto the front porch. The other serving girl was already outside holding the bay horse ready for him.

"G'bye, folks."

"Good day, Longarm."

Luncheon, Longarm thought as he rode toward the narrow, switchback trail that would take him down the face of the bluff to the valley floor. Interesting. Possibly damned well productive. And not at all what he'd expected, whatever that might've been.

# Chapter 19

It was well past the middle of the afternoon by the time Longarm returned to Cimarron City from the luncheon at The Folly. Late enough, he judged, that he could resume his phony search for a whore who didn't exist. Although if he didn't do any better at fooling the townspeople than he had Willard Sherman there wasn't much point in bothering with the charade.

Still, he had to assume that the colonel who lived atop the bluff was able to keep secrets.

He found the tenderloin district of the town—which pretty much accounted for the bulk of the business community here—and began knocking on doors. Most of them weren't open yet but at least the residents of the whorehouses were beginning to wake and stir. It was in the third place he visited that he began to smile.

"Edna?"

"Hello, Custis. Yes, it's really me. But I wouldn't have believed it was you either except that I was expecting you. Come in, dear. Let me get you something to drink. Are you hungry? Where have you . . . ?"

"Whoa," he said with a grin. "Slow down, Edna, we both got plenty of questions to ask an' answers t' hear." He stepped inside the whorehouse door, took the madam by the shoulders and stood there for a moment admiring her. "You look wonderful, Edna. You surely do." There was a fondness in his voice and tenderness in his eyes. "I swear you look younger'n the last time I saw you."

She smiled and he wasn't sure but thought he could detect a hint of moisture gathering bright and shiny in her pretty green eyes. "You look awful good too, Custis. You taken to the law since I seen you last. That's what I hear. A big time marshal all the way down here from Denver."

He nodded, smiled, allowed her to draw him inside the place, and push the door closed behind them.

Custis Long and Edna Walsh went back an awful long way. All the way back to where he'd been a pup still young enough to think he needed to prove himself to somebody— maybe to himself—and she was a slim, dewy-eyed girl fresh off a Kentucky tobacco field, on the run from demons she never talked about but demons serious enough that she would rather make her living by entertaining men at a dollar a bang than go back to where she came from.

Custis—there wasn't any Longarm then—got into a scrape to keep a drunk from carving on Edna's face one night. That had been—he had to think on it a bit before he could call it back to mind—that had been in Kansas. One of the cow towns. He disremembered just which one. It had been . . .

"Twelve years, Custis," Edna said. "It doesn't feel that long, does it?"

"Nope, it sure don't." He bent and kissed the cheek she offered him.

There had been a time when it was more than a cheek she gave him. There had been a time when Custis—he was young then and intense and not entirely sure that a man oughta take quite so many liberties with a woman's body unless he was willing to make an honest woman of her, never mind what the woman did for a living—would have expected more.

They'd lived together for a time there, not man and wife but just about as good as. Until the wet-behind-the-ears cowboy's money ran out and Edna so matter-of-factly said she was going back to work.

Oh, she was willing to keep on with Custis as her one and only boyfriend. But she'd been wanting to have him as her kept man, not a husband, wanted to dress him up and show him off and make sure he was the richest and most pampered kept man along the row. He could gamble or play or do whatever he wanted, she'd said. She would tend to business and provide the wherewithal for him to do it.

That hadn't much been to Custis's taste. And Miss Edna proved to be a more independent-minded and stubborn little slip of a thing than he'd ever suspected. She was willing to be his woman. But she was gonna hang onto her work too.

They'd argued about that. In the end they'd parted company. Longarm hadn't been sure until this very moment if they'd actually parted as friends or not.

He guessed now that they had. He smiled and gently squeezed her shoulders and once more lightly kissed her cheek. "I swear you still make my belly churn an' my cods hang heavy, Eddie. That ain't changed either."

Edna—Eddie was a pet name that had been spoken only in private between the two of them—blushed. He couldn't believe it. Except that he saw it for his own self. She stood right there in the whorehouse door and she blushed. "You shouldn't talk like that, Custis."

"No?"

She shook her head. "What you should do, dear, is come back to the kitchen. I haven't had my breakfast yet. Come join me, dear."

"All right." He trailed along behind her, content to admire the view from back there.

As a girl Edna had been on the scrawny side. As a woman she was lush. She had filled out and come into the promise that her youth suggested. She was a fine-looking figure of a woman now, narrow of waist and full of bosom and butt. Her copper-colored hair was pinned up in an elaborate do, and her pale green gown was expensively tailored. Edna seemed to be doing all right for herself. She had a peaches-and-cream complexion that never used to need any powders or rouges. Now she was wearing a little makeup, but Longarm would have been willing to bet that she didn't really need any artificial enhancements. Eddie herself should be enough to arouse any man who hadn't yet been dead more'n four days.

Certainly she was still capable of arousing him. He could feel the rising, swelling press of growing tumescence as they walked through an empty, musty-smelling parlor and on past to a kitchen where a tall, homely colored woman was tending a stove and half a dozen unpainted whores in cheap kimonos

74

were gathered around a rickety table. The ladies of the night looked pretty much like hell in the daylight. Funny how they could seem so attractive when the lights were low and the liquor was flowing.

"Girls, this is the gentleman I was just telling you about. This is my old and dear friend Marshal Custis Long."

"You knew I was in town then?"

"But of course, dear. If you hadn't found me in the course of your search, why, I would've come to find you. Naturally though we've all heard about why you are here. I intend to help you any way I can, Custis. That's a promise, dear."

There was a way Eddie could help, all right. But they'd discuss that later. In private. Longarm smiled. She patted his elbow and motioned him toward a seat at the foot of the big table.

"Martha, please go and tell the mister that we have a visitor," Eddie said crisply.

"Yes'm," the cook mumbled. She rearranged the pans on the stove toward the back of the hot surface, back toward where the heat would be less intense, and hurried away through a side door.

The mister. That meant. . . . Longarm's erection commenced to shrivel and fade into memory.

It was just as well that it had gone. Shortly the cook returned and with her a bleary-eyed, unshaven man in bare feet and unkempt trousers. He came out yawning and stumbling but frowned and squared his shoulders when he saw who the visitor was.

"Long," he growled.

"Do we . . . ?" Longarm had scarcely started the question when he clamped his jaw shut, biting the words off. "Harry Shelton." Jeez. It really was. Longarm hadn't recognized the son of a bitch at first. Harry had a paunch on him now and he was gray on top where before he'd been fit and dark and mean as the hounds of hell. Well, probably he still had the same shitty disposition. But that looked to be all that was the same with old Harry.

There'd been a time when Harry Shelton was a man Custis Long looked up to. Even wished he could pattern himself after. Then there was a time when Harry Shelton tried to compete with young Long for Edna's affections. Harry had lost that round. Along with several teeth and a fair amount of blood. Now it looked like Harry'd won the war even if he did lose that early battle.

"Long time, Harry."

"Not long enough," Shelton said.

"Don't be silly, dear. All that is a long time ago. Water under the bridge, ha ha. Sit down, darling. I was just going to offer Custis some breakfast. You know why he's come, of course. And you are the most knowledgeable man on the line, dear. I was hoping you could help Custis find this woman he's looking for."

Shelton took the chair at the head of the table and glared down the length of it at the man who so long ago had been his rival. "I could've taken you in a fair fight, you know. You sucker-punched me that time, Long. You know that as good as I do but I bet you aren't man enough to admit it."

Good heavens. The poor SOB was still pissed off about something that happened a dozen years back, Longarm realized.

"There was a time you could've taken me, Harry. I ain't scared to say that. It's true enough." That was what the dumb bastard wanted to hear, and it was a cheap enough pleasure to give him. Never mind mentioning that the day when Harry Shelton could've whupped Custis Long was when Harry was a mean-as-shit ten-year-old and Long was a babe in diapers. Never mind any of that.

Shelton grunted, apparently unsure of what to think or do now that the victory was so easily won.

Edna smiled. She seemed willing to believe that everything was fine now. She motioned for Martha to begin serving breakfast. Longarm wasn't hungry after the big meal at The Folly, but he knew he couldn't refuse to eat at Harry Shelton's table without risking a fuss with the idiot. He accepted coffee and some apple fritters that'd been rolled in sugar.

"Now tell us more about this woman you're looking for, Custis. We will help you any way we possibly can," Edna promised. "Won't we, dear?"

# Chapter 20

Harry Shelton bent over his bacon and fried taters like he hadn't heard the question. But his scowl said that he had. He was simply ignoring it.

"Darling," Edna persisted, "you were saying just last night that you thought Hannah Lou might have been this Helen Green person that Custis is looking for."

Longarm raised an eyebrow. Shelton continued to peer sullenly at his breakfast. "Hannah Lou?" Longarm asked. Although he suspected . . . hoped . . . he already knew who Eddie was talking about.

The woman returned her attention to Longarm. "A working girl, Custis. Not one of mine. No one knew her real name. But then of course we seldom do. She called herself Hannah Lou while she was here. Harry was saying as recently as last night that she might be the woman you are looking for here. The description fits. What little of it we heard, that is. And I know for a fact that she came here from Denver. She mentioned mutual friends there."

Again Longarm lifted an eyebrow in question.

"She didn't work for me, but when she first hit town she came here looking for a job. I turned her down, of course."

"Why was that a matter of course, Eddie?"

At mention of the nickname Shelton looked up from his meal with a darker scowl than ever.

"Hannah was a . . . how shall I put this? . . . she was getting old, Custis. Much too old to work in a house like this one. I have high standards, you know. I accept only the best. The only way I could have used a woman like Hannah would have been as a maid. In fact I offered to hire her as one of my maids. They come and go constantly, you understand. There is always work for a good maid who knows the business and can get along with the girls. But Hannah had an opium habit. She said she needed to earn more than a maid's pay. I suggested she talk with, well, never mind the gentleman's name. He, um, owns crib row. The important thing is that he allowed Hannah to rent one of the cribs. I understand she took to accepting those colored soldiers even though she was white. If you can imagine it. A white woman." Edna shuddered. "We have colored girls for that, you know. And Indians and whatever. But not the white girls. That simply shouldn't be done. Hannah knew better. Of course that only goes to show how far she'd sunk already, taking on those smelly, sweaty, awful coloreds." Edna didn't give thought that her own Negro cook was listening to all this. Or she just didn't care. Or it was even possible that she believed what she was saying so strongly that it never occurred to her that the attitude might give offense. Longarm idly wondered which of the many possibilities might be the truth of the matter.

"Obviously I need to talk with this Hannah," Longarm said. "Would you mind telling me where to find her?"

"Oh, didn't I tell you, Custis? She's dead."

"Dead?" He pretended not to have known.

"Suicide." Edna shrugged. "It's common enough, you know. Once the girls start going downhill. And poor Hannah had gone just about as low as anyone can. I can't say that anyone was surprised that she took her own life."

"Laudanum, I suppose," Longarm mused. He knew as well as anyone that an overdose of the readily available drug was the most common method of suicide among the soiled doves of Edna's chosen profession.

"Not Hannah, Custis. My, I can't imagine how much laudanum it would have taken to kill her. She was quite heavily addicted, you see. No, she chose to hang herself."

"Ugly."

"Yes, isn't it."

"Dumb bitch," Shelton muttered, joining the conversation for the first time.

"Pardon?"

"I said she was a dumb bitch. Hung herself but didn't get it right. Musta let herself down onto the rope easy instead o' dropping to make it quick and sure. Like letting yourself into a creek an inch at a time instead of jumping in and getting it over with. So she dangled there all blue in the face and strangling for who knows how long. Changed her damn mind about it, I can tell you that. I saw her when they cut her down. Her fingernails were all tore up from where she'd tried to pull the rope loose. But she was a fat pig. Too heavy to hold herself up one-handed so she could get some slack, I'd say." There was animation in Shelton's voice now. Almost an eagerness to discuss this particular topic, even with Custis Long. Apparently there was something about the death that pleased Harry Shelton. About death in general or about Hannah Lou's in particular, Longarm wondered? It occurred to him that Shelton might well be a member of the local vigilance committee. After all, it wasn't like the man had a schedule too busy to permit such voluntary community service work.

"Pity," Longarm observed.

Shelton waved a hand in dismissal of the expression of sympathy. "Ah, she was just another whore." No one else at the table, including Edna and her own string of whores, appeared to take offense at that, nor indeed to think there was anything remotely odd about it. It was as if the women themselves thought that whores were unworthy of sympathy.

"Pity I can't talk to her and find out if she was the woman I'm looking for," Longarm amended. Although that hadn't been his original meaning at all.

Shelton glanced at him, then looked back down without speaking. Suddenly remembering that he had a grudge with Long, perhaps.

"Could you tell me where her crib was?" Longarm asked.

"You won't find anything there," Edna said.

"Can't hurt to look." Hell, he was only going through the motions. At least so far as the dead woman's identity was concerned. The pity of it, and it was a true pity now that he thought of it, was that no one, not even himself as an officer of the law, really did care about the woman who had called herself Hannah Lou. Didn't care who she had been or how she had come to her fate in this dry and dreary little corner of nowhere that was Cimarron City. Nope, not even Deputy Long. All he wanted was to use the poor, dead bawd to gain information about something else. Being used casually and without consideration likely had been the total of the woman's experience when she was living and hadn't changed any now that she was dead and buried. And wouldn't that make for one hell of an epitaph, he thought, suddenly feeling as sour as Harry Shelton was acting.

"Are you sure you won't have something more to eat, Custis?"

"No thanks, Eddie." He'd used the nickname again without thinking. Again, though, there was a murderous glare sent his way from Harry Shelton's hooded eyes. Obviously Shelton resented any continuing degree of familiarity between Edna and Custis Long. It was something Longarm decided he'd really better try and keep in mind in the future. He wasn't afraid of Shelton, wouldn't have felt any need to back down from a dozen just like him, but there was seldom any purpose in goading a snake. "If you'd tell me where that crib is . . . ?"

"Martha, show Mr. Long what he wants," the whorehouse madam ordered.

"Yes'm." The cook/swamper/all around errand person put aside a dishrag, dried her hands, and was ready to lead the way outside by the time Longarm stood and mumbled his goodbyes.

# Chapter 21

"Got a cold, Martha?" he asked as the colored woman led him away from Edna's whorehouse and down an alley.

"What say, mister?"

"I asked if you had a cold. Because of the way you were sniffing."

"I was?"

He grinned. "Well, maybe it didn't so much sound like a head cold kind of sniff at that."

The woman sniffed again. More loudly this time. It was clear that what she was expressing was disgust.

"It was a long time ago that I could've thought of either one of those people as friends, Martha," Longarm said gently.

She gave him a searching look. Then visibly relaxed. "The sergeants say you aren't like most of your kind," she admitted. "They say you're more like the old captain. He's all right, you know. Fair. Doesn't matter to him about all that other stuff. Just what's right and what's wrong. They say maybe you're like that too."

"There are worse things that could be said about somebody," he observed.

"Ain't that the truth." They had reached the edge of a street running parallel to the one where Edna's whorehouse was sited. Martha paused there, not continuing out onto it. Longarm stopped beside her.

"If you need any help, mister . . ." She let the suggestion trail away into silence.

"I do," he acknowledged. "And I don't have to tell anybody where it comes from."

Martha sniffed again. Even louder this time. "That. Bah! I don't worry about that, mister. That woman, she don't pay me so much that I'm gonna worry about her getting mad. If she fires me somebody else will hire me. I get along. Always have."

"I believe you."

"Point is, mister, in a town like this, places like where I work, nobody sees a black face. Unless it's some nigger getting uppity, mind. Some shiny black soldier walk into a white man's bar or want to fuck a white whore, the white folks see that all right. See that and do something about it. But those of us as keeps our place and bobs our heads and shuffles out of the way when a white person walks by, why, we might as well be ghosts for all we're paid attention to." Martha smiled. "You tell me what you want to know, mister. I'll have every colored maid and cook and laundry boy in this town on the lookout for what you want."

Longarm smiled too. And told her what he wanted to know.

"I can't give you any answers now, mister. I just don't know none of that. But we'll all of us look to finding out."

"Thank you, Martha. Thank you very much."

She grunted, seemingly satisfied, and pointed out into the street and to her right. "Crib row, it's around there. Next two alleys you see. That Hannah Lou's, it was in the first alley, last door on your left. Second alley, that's where the colored soldiers are allowed. Best you stay out o' there, mister. Until the word goes around anyway, then it be all right for you to go wherever you want."

Longarm decided not to pursue the veiled hint that perhaps the colored community here was getting proddy in the wake of the assaults on the soldiers. That, he figured, could wait a bit longer. "Thanks," was all he said for the time being. He touched the brim of his Stetson in silent salute and strode out into the street.

The businesses facing the street here were all saloons and gaming houses. It was clear where the line was drawn between the playground for whites and the very similar one provided to rake in the payrolls of the Negro soldiers from

Good Enough. Every storefront on the block where Longarm now found himself carried a sign proclaiming Whites Only. The conspicuously posted signs ended at the mouth of the alley that held the cribs. Beyond that there was a store with the pawnbroker's ages-old three-ball symbol hanging over the door—neutral territory, Longarm judged—and past that the mouth of the other crib alley, the one that catered to the men from Camp Good Enough. Beyond that alley opening he could see more saloons and more gambling houses. Presumably those accepted colored patrons because he could see no signboards beside their doors like the Whites Only signs at this end of the short street.

Longarm shrugged—there are a good many things that can't be changed; a sensible man tries to figure out which things those are and then leave them be—and headed into the first alley. Last crib on the left, Martha had said. . . .

The place where a woman known as Hannah Lou worked and died was pretty much typical for an end-of-the-road whore grunting her way through her last years of commercial usefulness. It was a rickety, tiny thing built of poles and lathing. Pieces of canvas had been tacked over the otherwise open doorway and lone, unglazed window at the front. The place would be hell for cold in the winter and ovenlike in the heat of summer, Longarm knew. But then it was only a whore that would live there.

Longarm tapped on the lathing beside the doorway and cleared his throat. He heard no sound from within. Presumably then no replacement had been found yet to rent it now that Hannah Lou was dead. He pushed the stiff canvas aside and looked inside.

The crib was roughly eight feet deep and six feet wide. A shelflike bench had been built across the full width of the back wall, and a grass-stuffed mattress ticking lay on it to serve as the bed that was the primary purpose of the structure. In this case the "bed" was no mere piece of furniture but the most stout and solid part of the structure itself. Sensible, Longarm conceded. There wasn't any amount of thrashing and banging could break a bed like that.

The front of the room held a straight-backed wooden chair and a wooden table with a pitcher and basin on it. A pair of wrought-iron candle holders had been spiked into the walls, one above the bed and the other beside the door. Pegs had been driven into the walls also to serve as a wardrobe or armoire, and an ash-strewn set of indentations in the dirt floor showed that a small stove had been in place there at some time in the past. Other marks in the dirt indicated that a trunk or chest had been in the crib too, but there was no sign of it now.

There was, in fact, no sign at all of the woman who had called herself Hannah Lou. No clothes, no toiletries, not even any sheet or blankets on the mattress ticking. The place was barren of personality, the only scrap of human touch visible being a cigar butt that had been ground into the dirt in front of the straight chair. Everything else, every article that Hannah Lou may have owned, had been stripped from the crib and carried away down to and including the candles that should have been in the holders. The iron candle holders were both empty now.

It was damned lucky, Longarm decided, that he didn't actually need to learn much about the woman who had died here.

He pulled out a cheroot and lighted it, then spent another moment examining the ceiling of the place. Two beams of squared timber were run as stringers down the length of the block of cribs. It was impossible to tell where the rope might have been placed to hang Hannah Lou or where the chair had been. Scrape marks on the floor gave no clue to that information. For sure, though, the death by slow strangulation that Harry Shelton had described would have been a shitty way to die. Surely after suffering through that, and the shitty life that led to the dying, anyone should have been entitled to more in the way of memory than this, should have left some small sign that a living, breathing person had passed this way. Yet the woman known as Hannah Lou seemed to have left no mark whatsoever, neither of her living nor of her dying.

Longarm grunted, saddened on behalf of the unmourned old bawd, and turned away. He had come here to work, dammit, not to ponder stupidly maudlin thoughts.

He stepped outside and walked the few paces to the end of the alley. All the cribs on either side of the short alley were built together, one long and narrow structure on each side with walls to chop them into the six-foot crib sections. At this time of afternoon all of them were closed, canvas or wooden doors shut to block out the sun. Soon enough it would come dark and the whores would waken and begin to hawk themselves on the open market. That would commence at dark or earlier if customers began to arrive sooner in search of relief for their urges.

There were—he counted—ten cribs on each side of the alley. There was no way he could tell how many of the total of twenty were occupied at the moment.

Crib row ended at the blank, windowless back end of a building that presumably faced onto the next business block over. From the alley here Longarm could not tell what the building was.

Between the cribs and that building, though, there was a narrow gap. Whoever built the cribs did not actually connect them to the other structure. A gap of perhaps two feet was left between them. And that gap, Longarm saw, connected with the next crib alley over, the one where the colored troops were free to trade. If a man didn't mind scrunching sideways for the required distance he could gain access to the back of the alley—that is, to Hannah Lou's crib there at the end—without having to openly come in from the street.

A customer could sure do that, Longarm saw.

He walked over to the other side of the narrow alley and peered behind the right-hand row of cribs. There was a similar gap on that side. Meaning that a Negro soldier could have approached Hannah Lou's workplace from the one side. Or anybody else could have come into the alley unseen from this other side. Wherever it led.

On an impulse, Longarm tapped the ash off the tip of his cheroot, turned sideways and edged his way in behind the crib that faced Hannah Lou's across the alley. Might be mildly interesting, he thought, to see just what lay in that direction. The direction where a white man—a vigilante, say—could've come from the night Hannah Lou died so hard and ugly.

# Chapter 22

Longarm stepped out of the gap into a tiny, trash-strewn courtyard sort of arrangement that was surrounded by the back walls of four, five, however many business buildings in the block. The purpose of the open area was easy enough to see. A pair of outhouses occupied most of the available space, and narrow paths showed plain amid the weeds and the litter, the paths branching off toward the back doors of the nearby buildings.

There were no obvious clues to show what the businesses were that circled so tight around this area of shared shitters. Normally one would expect to find outhouses in areas used for loading docks and the like, areas that could be expected to show signs of what lay beyond the blank walls, but the makeshift buildings of Cimarron City had been allowed to grow up in a slapdash, haphazard manner and no such planning had been bothered with. The one building Longarm was sure of was the one that sat next to the line of cribs. That one was a saloon. He followed the path that led to it and let himself in the back way. Immediately he was surrounded by the sharp, biting odors of stale beer and fresh smoke. A saloon, he reflected, has a smell like no other sort of place in the world. Not a bad smell either. Just distinctive. The sounds and the feelings within a beer joint will change with the time of day and the mood of the patrons, change just as regular as the tides. But the smell of such a place never varies. He drew deep on his cheroot and followed a short, dark hallway forward to the main room.

"Longarm!" a loud and happy voice greeted him as soon as he stepped out of the hall.

"Charley," he returned, altering direction so he could join his big, cheerful friend at the bar. "What brings you here so early?"

"Why, I came in t' buy you a beer, Longarm," Charley said with a grin. "Got done working and figured I owed myself one. Specially since I still got so many aches to drown." He chuckled and rubbed his butt. Still and all, though, he looked and moved just fine for a man who'd been in a kicking contest with a horse. Longarm wasn't so sure he would be feeling as chipper as Charley obviously was if the experience had been his.

"Then whyn't I buy you one instead," Longarm insisted. "Since that mare was only doing my work for me anyhow."

Charley guffawed and by way of compromise called for a pair of mugs for each of them. Longarm propped an elbow on the bar beside the man and offered him a smoke, lighting it from the stub of his own nearly spent cheroot.

"You doin' any good, Longarm?"

"Not really. Somebody was tellin' me that the woman I want might've been some whore that was killed here recent."

Charley frowned in concentration, then nodded. "I know the one you mean. Cheap, ugly ol' fat thing, she was. Over in the cribs. Some son of a bitch strung her up one night an' made it look like she done it herself. But she never."

"No?" Until now everyone Longarm heard speak of Hannah Lou's death had gone along with the pretense that it was suicide.

"Naw, o' course not. Hell, she was makin' money here. Why would she hang herself when she was doing the best she'd done in years? Maybe ever."

"You sure about this, Charley?"

"Oh, hell yes. That woman was screwin' the niggers at two bucks a throw. Everybody knew it."

"And you say somebody killed her for it?"

"Oh, I dunno that that's why they kilt her. Prob'ly not would be my guess. I mean, it wasn't no white guy that kilt her or I'd've heard about it by now. Which means it was one of them nigger soldiers that done her. Got mad at her 'bout something. Or, hell, just wanted to kill him a white woman, I dunno. Not that anybody around here cares, y'see. Not about a woman like that. We got better things to worry about than some two-bit hoor that fucks niggers."

"I see," Longarm said. Although he didn't. "Charley, are you pretty sure it wasn't some white who killed that woman? Sure it couldn't have been, like, a vigilance committee or the Ku Kluxers?"

Charley snorted and tipped his mug high to drain the last swallow out of that one. He smacked his lips and reached for his next mug. "Longarm, you and me are friends. I wouldn't steer you wrong. If it was anything like you just said I damn well guarantee you I'd know about it. Shit, Longarm, if it was anything like that, I woulda been *in* on it. But it wasn't. If it was, friend, I'd say so. Or not say nothing at all if I thought that was best. But I wouldn't lie to you about it. And I'm telling you as one friend to another that it wasn't no vigilance committee and it wasn't no Ku Klux Klan . . . which we do have here, sure, but which wasn't busy that particular night . . . and far as I've heard it wasn't any white man doing it on his own neither. I can promise you on the first two things an' believe but can't actual prove that it wasn't some lone guy that was pissed off at her. Like I said, I'm sure I'd've heard if it was. Okay?"

Longarm grunted. And motioned to the bartender for another couple rounds.

This was damn-all interesting. Longarm had the distinct impression that his good and true pal Charley was telling the exact and literal truth to him. That Hannah Lou had not died the way Captain Denis and the men at Camp Good Enough believed.

"You say there is a KKK chapter here, Charley?"

"Sure. It's a protective society, like. I'm a member my own self. You wanta join, Longarm?"

"Uh, no thanks."

"Wouldn't be anything happening at our meetings that we wouldn't let an officer o' the law see. In fact, there's plenty officers that do belong. Not in this chapter here particularly but some places."

"I know that."

"We figure to tend to our own knitting. Just as long as them soldiers stay in their place."

"And what is their place, Charley?"

"You see the way it is on the street here. They got that end, we got this end. No need for any trouble long as it stays apart like that. And I got to say, them nigger boys out at the fort haven't been sneaking around the houses where respectable folks live or nothing like that. Though we'd heard this bunch gave a lot o' trouble where they come from before here, raping decent women and like that. That's why we formed us a Klan chapter. But they've kept t' their own place so far. We won't do nothing as long as that's so."

Longarm grunted. "And there isn't any other group? No vigilance committee or anything like that?"

"I'm telling you, Longarm, there couldn't be without me knowing. I mean, shit, our Klan chapter would *be* the committee if there was gonna be one."

"And you're sure you'd know everything that's going on, Charley? The officers wouldn't keep secrets from the members, maybe?"

Charley laughed. "Longarm, ol' friend, just who 'n hell d'you think is the Grand Dragon here?"

"Oh."

So much for theories and figuring things out without having all the facts, Longarm conceded. "Charley, you're all right. I'm glad I run inta you this afternoon."

"You ain't fixing to leave are you?"

"Got to. But I'll be around town a while longer. I wouldn't go off any place without getting together and hoisting a few more."

"That's a promise," Charley insisted.

"Damn right," Longarm agreed. He dropped a silver dollar on the bar, enough to pay for everything they'd ordered and a helluva lot more yet to come, and walked out into the slanting sunlight of the late afternoon. He squinted toward the west. The way he calculated it, he still had time to collect his horse and get back to Good Enough in time for supper at the officers' mess.

# Chapter 23

"If you'd excuse us, sir?"

"Very well, Wyche. Carry on."

The lieutenant nodded first to his commanding officer then to the visitor at the mess before he turned and hurried off to whatever nocturnal pursuit had already enticed the other junior officers away. Brandy and coffee hadn't even been served yet and already the mess tent was deserted except for Captain Denis and Longarm. At least Wyche had had the courtesy to request permission to withdraw. The others had simply gobbled their meals and hurried off into the newly fallen night. Busy boys, Longarm thought with a frown. Come morning they would all be hung over. Which was, fortunately, neither his responsibility nor his concern.

"Cigar, Longarm?"

"Thank you, Hal." The stogie was plump and pale but of mediocre quality, the sort of smoke that could be bought cheaply in large quantity, exactly the sort of thing one might expect to find in a junior officers' mess. Longarm accepted the offer without a murmur, ignoring his own much superior cheroots in favor of good manners.

"Are you making any progress with our problem, Longarm?" Denis asked after the coffee had been poured and the brandy snifters warmed.

"Not really," Longarm conceded. He took a sip of the brandy. It too leaned more toward economy than quality, and he was no fancier of brandy to begin with. Still, Hal Denis seemed pleased to be able to enjoy civilized amenities with someone who was not trying to escape from his company.

Putting up with brandy and a cheap stogie were small prices to pay in exchange for giving the officer the pleasure of acting the gracious host. "Only thing I've learned in town so far is that nobody there seems t' know anything about this vigilante bunch you talked about. Yet your men tell you there is such, right?"

"They do. Although I cannot vouch for that information, Longarm. I think I told you that already. I repeated rumor and common belief. Strict adherence to fact is not necessary in either of those categories."

Longarm nodded and took another sip of the brandy. "Not that it matters so much, I suppose." He smiled. "Anyway, we don't wanta spoil the evening talking shop." He crossed his legs and leaned back. "Tell me, Hal, you been with this outfit very long?"

"That depends on what you think is a long time, doesn't it? Would six years qualify as long?"

"Would t' me. And that's the truth."

"For a military officer, Longarm, six years is barely enough time to unpack. Some of us, those of us who are not reaching for the stars, tend to stay with our units for many many years, sometimes for entire careers."

Longarm nodded. That was particularly true with senior enlisted personnel, he knew. It occurred to him that Hal Denis might be a former enlisted man himself, risen from the ranks to command but now stagnant.

"And frankly, Longarm, it would be my hope that I am allowed to remain with these men for the remainder of my service. In spite of everything I would have to admit to being comfortable in my situation. I like the job and I like the people."

"And the place?"

Denis shrugged. "To a soldier, place hardly matters. We move about. The unit remains a whole regardless of where it happens to pitch its tents."

"So you wouldn't mind moving again?"

"Certainly not. Can I refresh your drink there? Ring for more coffee? No? In fact, Longarm, I suspect we could be moving again very soon. You'll notice I haven't been in any hurry to erect permanent structures here. The placement of

Good Enough has been disputed from the beginning. Lord only knows why, but there has been a certain level of political groundswell opposing the location here. Someone, for whatever reason, seems to want us moved further east into the Indian Territories. Although in order to find reliable water sources to the east, enough to provide for our Remount function, we would have to be impossibly far away from the national cattle road. Not that it seems to need any attention at the moment but the fact remains that guarding the Ogallala cattle road is one of our assigned duties. That is why I've resisted the pressures for us to move. This is the only point I'm aware of that allows us to serve all the functions that are asked of us."

"Those bein' t' guard the Ogallala and t' raise and break Remount horses and t' keep station in case there's a hostile reservation break off the I.T."

"Exactly."

"No orders to move yet though, right?"

"None forthcoming that I am aware of. But one never knows."

"An' before you came to Good Enough?"

"Oh, goodness. There have been so many." There was something in Denis's voice that told Longarm the man's memories were for the most part very pleasant ones. "Forts Quitman, Davis, Taylor. Immediately before we came here we were at Concho. You've heard of it?"

"O' course. Down Texas way just like the rest of the places you mentioned."

Denis puffed on his stogie for a moment, wreathing his head in pale smoke. "I won't say my men were totally accepted there, of course. They couldn't expect that anywhere, I suppose. But at least the conditions at those posts had been such that the presence of soldiers in blue coats, even dark-skinned soldiers in blue coats, was welcomed by the settlers. There has been so much fighting there, you know. With the Comanche and the Kiowa and the Apache. And of course with Mexican bandits and revolutionaries. Then there have been gangs of plain old plug-uglies and filibusters and incursionists. Stormy country, that. But they've long appreciated the help they received from colored soldiers.

My men were sorry to be ordered away."

"I've been to Concho but not in a long time. There's a town there now, is there?"

"Oh, yes. You know how that is. Just like here. Once there is a post and a payroll, civilian interests move in also. Quite often a town grows up close by a fort. Look at Dodge City. Nowadays people tend to think of it solely as a town and forget that it was the fort that created the community, not the other way 'round."

"But the folks down there at Concho got along with your boys, Hal?"

"Very well. Nothing is perfect, of course, but I would say there was very little friction between my men and the civilian community."

"And your boys were well-behaved down there?"

Denis snorted. "I may not seem much to you, Longarm, but let me assure you, my men do not misbehave. I run a tighter command than is apparent. Thanks largely to my sergeants, I am aware of any problem involving my people. And I'm not hesitant about punishment."

"Even serious stuff?"

"You are welcome to inspect the records of my command if you wish, sir." Denis sounded like he was willing to become testy if his guest pursued this line of conversation much further. "Our records of court martials date back all the way to the formation of the unit."

"No need t' get excited, Hal. I was just wondering. You know."

"No, sir, I do not know what you are driving at. I do not, sir." At this point the captain was sitting bolt upright on his chair, ramrod stiff and eyes flashing.

"Look, Hal, I'm sorry. The truth is, I heard a rumor. In town. Something about your boys having been in lots o' trouble before they came here. Rape, robbery, that sort o' thing."

"Damn!" Denis blurted. He came off his chair in a rush and with a show of considerable agitation began pacing back and forth, his gait lopsided and rolling because of his one bad leg. "Damn," he repeated. "The injustice of it. The *indecency* of subjecting these good men to such calumny.

93

The . . . the . . ." He sputtered and fumed, apparently unable to think of a term strong enough to convey his disgust.

"Whoa. Calm down, Hal. It was only a rumor. Wouldn't you rather a person asked outright instead o' taking it at face value?"

"Of course. Of course I would. But the indecency of it, the indignity, the . . . the . . . the . . ."

"It's okay, Hal. I believe you."

"Yes, but . . . Dammit, Longarm, there has not been one single charge of serious nature against my men in at least five years. And that court martial involved military property only. Several of my people were in collusion with a post trader who was stealing rations and selling them back to the men out of company funds. The trader's license was revoked and the men who were involved with him were given dishonorable discharges. But beyond that . . . why, there hasn't been anything involving a civilian, nothing more serious than a fistfight, in all the time I have been with this unit. Rape, sir? Believe me, any colored soldier who raped a white woman in Texas would be hanged before military justice had its crack at him. There simply has been none of that. My men take pride in themselves, Longarm. They would police themselves against any member of the unit who might bring dishonor onto the rest. No, sir, I categorically refute those rumors. Never, sir. Not in this command. Why . . ."

Hal Denis was off and running, marching back and forth, blustering and fuming aloud, waving his arms wildly. He got redder and redder in the face until Longarm commenced to worry about the man's health, fearful the army captain might suffer an attack of acute apoplexy and keel over before he could calm himself.

Longarm was almost sorry he'd brought the subject up.

But not really.

He was, in fact, finding Hal Denis's indignation almighty interesting.

# Chapter 24

The government bay ate up the distance to town at a swift and fluid jog that was as comfortable as sitting on a rocking chair. It was well past dark by the time Longarm reached the outskirts of Cimarron City, but it wasn't really late. There would be plenty of time for him to find Charley again for another conversation. And handle the few other things he wanted to take care of during the evening.

His first stop was at Edna and Harry's whorehouse. He tied the horse out front with a good many others and let himself in through a door that was already ajar. At this hour the place was brightly lighted and abuzz with activity. The only people in the parlor were men who were drinking and talking and likely were waiting for their turns with the ladies of their choice. Longarm could think of worse ways in which a man might spend his leisure time, actually.

"Sign up over there, mister," someone called out helpfully.

"If you can't read," another voice added, "tell the piana player."

The piano player was taking a break at the moment, but Longarm had no trouble identifying him when he stepped out of the door that led back to the kitchen. The piano player was a lanky Negro, definitely not the sort who would be welcomed among the clientele here, but good enough as an employee if he could be hired cheap.

"Lawzy, suh, a fine-lookin' gennelmun such as yo'self, I sho' woulda thought you'all could read an' 'rat an' cipher, suh," the piano player drawled in a mush-mouthed accent when Longarm approached him. "But you'all gots a long wait t'nigh', suh. We's s' busy, suh, dat e'en Miss Edna full up t'nigh', suh. I sho' be sorry, suh. But can I put you'all down fo' the firs' 'vailable young lady, suh?"

Longarm found it interesting that Edna still lent a hand—or whatever—when things got busy. But that wasn't who he'd come here to see. "Thanks, but I'm looking for Martha."

The piano player's smile flickered. When it came back it seemed somewhat on the sickly side. "Dat Marth', suh, she don' entertain no gennelman callers, suh. Please you t' go away now, suh?"

"I know Martha isn't one of the, um, working girls, friend. I only need to speak with her for a moment."

The piano player gave up the effort of forcing a smile that couldn't be believed anyway. "She ain' done nothin' wrong, suh. I sure 'bout dat."

"I only need to speak with her," Longarm repeated. He started past the piano player, heading into the kitchen.

The thin black man stood his ground for a moment, blocking the door he had just exited. Then, reluctantly, he stepped aside.

"Excuse me," Longarm said. The piano player followed close behind when Longarm entered the kitchen. "Good evening, Martha." He smiled and removed his Stetson.

Martha was busy at a sideboard preparing what looked to be plates of bite-sized snacks to send out to the parlor. When she saw Longarm she returned the smile and to the piano player said, "This is the man I was telling you about, Rastus. This is Marshal Long."

"Rastus?" Longarm asked of a slightly sheepish looking piano player.

"It's a long story, Marshal. Believe me, you don't want to hear it." He grinned. "But that old woman over there, she's heard about it plenty. And that, sir, is a promise." He extended his hand to Longarm and corrected the teasing impression Martha had made. "I'm George Freeman, Marshal."

"Custis Long, Mr. Freeman," Longarm said, accepting the handshake. "But my friends call me Longarm."

"Fair enough, Longarm. I'm George." In the kitchen now George Freeman had only the faintest softly sibilant accent,

Longarm noticed with some amusement.

"What can we do for you, Longarm?" Martha asked.

"I was wondering if you've learned anything since we spoke this afternoon," he said.

"Not yet, but I've put the word out. Or rather ol' Rastus there did it for me." She winked, and George Freeman laughed. "Is there a problem?" Martha asked.

"No, no problem. I was just in town and thought I'd stop by while I had the chance." Which was true enough as far as it went, never mind that it was far from being all of the truth. "By the way," Longarm added, "has either of you heard anything about the existence of a vigilance committee here in town?"

"Of course," Freeman said.

Longarm raised an eyebrow. Martha picked up her plate of hors d'oeuvres and brought it across the room, pushing it into George's hands. "You better get in there, honey,'fore you get yourself in trouble. If the marshal needs anything I can't supply I'll fetch you back in here."

"You're right. But I hate to admit it." Freeman leaned forward to give Martha a brief kiss on the cheek, then went back out to the waiting customers. A few moments later the sound of a slightly off-key piano could be heard through the thin wall. Martha winced. "That man surely does wish there was a piano tuner in this town," she said. "Come sit, Longarm, and let me get us some coffee. Or would you rather have something stronger?"

"Coffee will be fine, thanks."

"A bite of something to eat with it?"

"Just the coffee, thank you."

Martha brought two cups to the table and joined him. "Now. You asked about the vigilantes."

"That's right."

"If you need to know which men are part of the committee, Longarm, I'm afraid I can't tell you. And I know George couldn't either. Lord knows we've discussed this between ourselves often enough. The idea of a vigilance committee is frightening enough at any time. It's worse when it's whites against blacks."

"More frightening than the KKK?" Longarm asked.

"In this town at this time, yes," Martha responded. "The Klan here . . . we do know about them, you understand . . . they're really a bunch of silly men who like to drink corn whiskey and talk dirty, like boys trying to play at being grownup. But they aren't really as mean as they think they are, you see. George and I know what the genuine article can be, Longarm. We've seen lynch mobs in our time. And felt the sting of Klansmen's whips. But that isn't what you have here in Cimarron City. The Klan here," she shrugged, "we don't like them or anything about them. But we know who they are and what they are about. We know how to adapt, how to cope. We can live with the people in the Klan here. Here it's the vigilance committee we worry about. Because all we know about them is that they exist. And that they hate niggers and want all of us gone from their lives. Or at least put securely into our places. Maybe then there would be some small amount of room for us in their lily white lives."

"Interesting that your voice doesn't show any bitterness, Martha. You say those words but you don't sound bitter."

"That's because I'm not bitter, Longarm. I'm no young-ster, you see. I have lived, and I have learned. I left bitterness behind someplace. What I like to think I am is a realist." Her expression softened. "And hopefully a survivor."

"I hope so too." He took a sip of the coffee. "It's kinda surprising that there could be a committee of vigilance and neither you nor the Klan know about it."

"Oh, they know about it all right. This isn't so big a town for it to be otherwise. It takes men with special kinds of hate to belong to either of those groups. Surely most who belong to one would also belong to the other. I mean, the Klan, it's partially a social thing, you know. Lots of men regard it like it's a fraternity or a lodge, that sort of thing. Those white men like to parade around in their hoods and drink with the boys and think they're rough and tough so they can work up to coming in here and doing things with the whores that they wouldn't never think of do-ing with their wives. That kind wouldn't want to get in-volved with a vigilance bunch. But then there's a hard core of men in the Klan that really despise other men . . . and women . . .because of skin color. They want to do us hurt because we aren't the same as them. And that is the bunch that would also belong to the vigilantes. But I have to believe that nearly all the vigilantes, all the really and truly mean ones that is, would first belong to the Klan."

"I see what you mean. It makes sense," Longarm conceded. He smiled. "You've given this a great deal of thought, obviously. You're a bright woman, Mrs. Freeman."

She looked pleased but brushed the compliment away. "I'm only spouting back what that damned Rastus tells me."

"I hope you'll forgive me if I don't quite believe that, Mrs. Freeman. And if I may say so, George Freeman is a very lucky man." He lifted his coffee cup toward her in salute. Longarm wasn't sure—the lighting in the kitchen wasn't any great shakes, and Martha was plenty dark to begin with—but he thought the woman blushed this time.

Longarm would have talked with Martha longer, but the side door swung open and banged against the wall. Harry Shelton stumbled in. He was unsteady on his feet, and his hair was wildly mussed. The man looked like he'd spent the full time trying to crawl inside a whiskey bottle since Longarm last saw him earlier in the day.

"Long!" It was more snarl than acknowledgement. Certainly it was not a welcome. "You sonuvabitch."

Longarm chose to ignore that.

"You wanta fuck my wife, you sonuvabitch, you pay firs'. You hear me, Long? You pay firs', you bastard." Shelton reeled, catching himself barely in time to avoid toppling over, then reeled again and collided with the wall. Martha hurriedly left the table and went to assist her boss's fancy man. She slipped beneath a limp arm and supported him over to the chair she had just vacated. Harry Shelton snorted, belched once, and reached for Martha's coffee cup. He took a long swallow and smacked his lips. "That's good. Jus' what I needed." He belched again.

Obviously Harry hadn't noticed that Longarm and Martha were in conversation when he came in. Hadn't noticed either that it was her cup he was drinking from. Longarm suspected Harry would have been aghast if he had known. Not that

Longarm was gonna correct him on the subject. And from the sparkle of amusement that was almost but not quite hidden deep inside Martha's dark eyes he doubted she was likely to say anything either. Harry took another swallow, losing some of it down his chin and onto his already stained shirt front. "You sonuvabitch," he repeated from a distance close enough that Longarm could smell the hot stink of the whiskey on Harry's breath.

At that moment Longarm disliked Harry Shelton enough that he damn near challenged him to repeat his comment once he sobered up.

But then there is never any point in trying to talk to a drunk. Longarm scowled and stood. "Good night, Martha. Thank you for the coffee."

"Good night, Longarm."

"I don't want to bother George while he's working." The sound of the piano proved that George was busy at the moment. "Please tell him goodbye for me. And that it was a pleasure meeting him. I'm proud t' know the both of you."

Martha glanced toward Harry, who seemed oblivious to his surroundings, and winked at Longarm. "I'll tell him. And thank you."

Longarm turned to the door.

"Tha's righ' you sonuvabitch. Run 'way from me."

Longarm strode out of the room without bothering to look back.

# Chapter 25

Longarm turned to his right and started down the row of saloons looking for his good and true pal Charley. Longarm definitely needed to find him again and ask a few questions to clear something up. There was something the man had said earlier. . . .

"Nope, not in here, mister. Try next door."

"Right. Thanks."

"No, but he was in a little while ago. You might try next door."

It was like that in one place after another. Everyone knew Charley. For that matter, nearly everyone knew Longarm by now. Most admitted to having seen Charley earlier in the evening. No one seemed to know where he was at the moment. Longarm shrugged and made his way along the row, finally coming close to the line of demarcation that separated the play area for whites, the saloons and gaming halls and whorehouses, from the similar establishments that were set aside for the Negro soldiers from Camp Good Enough.

About the only difference that Longarm could see was in the color of the men down that way. The services were very much the same.

No point in looking for the head of the local KKK down that way, though. Charley would be found somewhere in this end of town if he was still on his evening's prowl. Longarm figured to keep marching on until he had covered all the possibilities.

He stopped in at one more saloon—he had long since discovered that there didn't seem to be a single place in the town that stocked a decent grade of rye whiskey—then went outside and paused to light a cheroot, bending his head to the flare of his match and drawing deep of the smoke. He shook the match out and tossed it away.

As he was doing so a sheet of flame blossomed in the mouth of an alley across the street.

The bright, yellow-gold flower of fire had a long spike in the center of it. And that fiery, lead-tipped spear was pointed square at Longarm. The sight of the flame was accompanied by the roar of a gunshot half a heartbeat later.

Too late to do any good but unable to resist the impulse, Longarm ducked.

By that time the slug from the ambusher's gun had already buried itself in the boards that sheathed the false front of the saloon Longarm just left.

He ducked instinctively, and his hand swept the big double action Colt out of his crossdraw holster.

Longarm's return fire spat across the street and into the alley almost before the echoing sound of the first gunshot died away.

He triggered three fast, searching rounds into the shadowy mouth of the alley, then he spun and darted back the way he'd just come.

It would've been heroic as all hell to charge straight across into that alley with his gun blazing and a gleam in his eye.

It also would have been dumb as shit. If the ambusher hadn't waited around he was gone by now. If he was still waiting there then he would've had a chance to correct his first mistake and take a second, perhaps better aimed shot while Longarm was out in the street with no cover for yards in any direction and with the light of all too many lamps spilling out of every building in this part of town.

It graveled Longarm to do it, but he slid out of sight just as quick as he could manage.

"I thought you'd left a'ready," the bartender said when Longarm returned to the saloon he'd so recently left.

"I did."

The man eyed the revolver the tall deputy was still holding. "That was you shooting out in the street, huh?"

"Yes, it was."

"See a snake or somethin'?"

"Something like that."

The barman shrugged. "So what can I get you, Marshal?"

"Rye."

"Thought you said you didn't like the brand I got."

"That's what I said all right." Longarm was becoming peeved with the fellow, and some of that must have been apparent in the tone of his voice. The bartender winced and reached for the bottle of poor rye without further comment. Longarm scowled and reloaded his Colt.

He would give it ten minutes, he figured. That would be time enough for the ambusher to bleed to death in the unlikely event that one of Longarm's blind shots had tagged him. Or to get the hell gone if that was what he intended.

Longarm wasn't all that worried about which way it shook out. If the SOB wasn't dead yet, well, Longarm figured he had a better than fair idea of where to go look for him.

Ten minutes, he told himself. He took a puff on his cheroot and tossed back the bar whiskey. The smoke tasted the better by far. On the other hand, even poor whiskey can put some warmth into a man's belly.

"Once more," Longarm said. The bartender poured without comment and scurried quickly away.

# Chapter 26

Close inspection with a borrowed lantern showed no blood stains or any other sign that the shooter had been hit. Or even that anyone had been in the alley. Not that Longarm really expected to find anything. And not that he was very much concerned about being able to find the ambusher now.

The way he figured it, it pretty much had to be that poor son of a bitch Harry Shelton who shot at him. Longarm couldn't think of anybody else in Cimarron City who might have a hard-on for him. Hell, he was even good buddies with the Ku Klux Klan here. And a committee of vigilance—if there was such a thing here, and wasn't that very much in doubt—surely wouldn't be stupid enough to try and gun down a U.S. marshal. If there was anything in the world that would be calculated to draw both attention and wrath, that would have to be it. So, no, Longarm didn't think a vigilante crowd could've been responsible for the shooting. If, that is, there was such a bunch in the town.

All of which left Edna's poor, dumb, jealous asshole Harry as the only likely culprit.

What pissed Longarm off—aside from having been shot at, that is—was that now old Harry would convince himself, was absolutely sure to, that Deputy Long was arresting him because Longarm still wanted Edna and wanted to get Harry out of the way. That was gonna happen inside Harry's half-pickled brain; Longarm could feel it in his bones just as sure as he was standing there. Arresting the silly SOB would only encourage him in his mistaken beliefs. In many ways Longarm hated to have to go and do it.

But dammit, he couldn't allow Shelton or anybody else to stagger around taking potshots at United States deputy marshals. That wasn't the sort of habit one wants to encourage.

With a sigh and a bit of grumbling reluctance, Longarm returned the lantern to its owner and strode off in the direction of the whorehouse.

Edna's was even busier this time than it had been earlier. The parlor was full of men who were waiting for their turn at a woman. Harry Shelton was not among them, though. Longarm nodded a howdy to George Freeman at the piano and inclined his head toward the kitchen, receiving a nod of approval from Freeman. Longarm continued on into the back. He found Martha Freeman bent over a copper-lined sink, up to her elbows in soap suds. She was busy washing a small mountain of glassware that had already been dirtied by the customers out front and likely would be cycled through at least once more before the night was over. The gentlemen of Cimarron City were a horny and a well-lubricated crowd.

"Hello again," Martha greeted. "What brings us the pleasure of your company so soon again, Longarm?"

"I'm looking for Harry, Martha."

She made a face and clucked softly to herself. But she didn't actually *say* anything about her employer. Or employer's boyfriend, beau, lover, whatever.

Longarm was already moving toward the side door that presumably led into the living quarters Harry and Edna shared.

"He isn't here, Longarm. The mister, he left a while ago, not too long after you went out earlier."

"He isn't back yet?"

"No."

"You're sure?"

"Real sure," she said. "Mister Harry never comes in through the front. That door right there, that's the one he always uses. I been here the whole time since you been gone, Longarm. He couldn't 've come back without me knowing."

Longarm frowned. "Any idea where I might find him now?"

This time both Martha's expression and her tone of voice betrayed her thoughts about Shelton. "By now, Longarm, I'd say that man be passed out cold and laying on the ground someplace. He was drinking before you got here and was drinking worse after you left. Couldn't no human person hold that much likker and still be on his feet this long. Not even him. You want him, Longarm, you best start looking underneath porches and into alleys. That'd be your best bet."

Longarm wasn't especially amazed by this news. A man like Harry would have to be right thoroughly soused in order to work up nerve enough for a shooting. Even for something as safe as a hit and run backshooting attempt at night. Harry Shelton hadn't had the makings of a gunman worth worrying about even when he'd been young and dry. As a middle-aged drunk, what little nerve he might once have had was long since gone and forgotten.

"Thanks, Martha." He smiled and tipped the brim of his Stetson to her. Since he was already standing beside the back door he let himself out that way rather than go back out through the crowd of customers. For some reason he would rather not run into Edna tonight anyway.

Once outside he took a long, deep breath of the clean, cool night air. It smelled an awful lot better out here than it had in the whorehouse.

Longarm trimmed and lighted a cheroot while he thought over his options. The simple truth was that by now Martha was probably right and Harry probably was passed out cold someplace. It wouldn't serve much purpose to drag him into whatever passed for a jail in town. He'd likely only puke on the floor and somebody else would have to clean up after him. Better to wait until morning, Longarm concluded. He could look Harry up then and see if the man still wanted to take a shot at him.

And Longarm could decide then if he wanted to bother arresting the dumb SOB. Arresting Harry wouldn't accomplish much. But then neither would letting him go. Dammit.

One nice thing. It wasn't something that absolutely had to be decided on tonight. For a change Longarm had the luxury of being able to sleep on a problem and see if it sorted itself out overnight.

Thinking about sleeping on it . . . He yawned and ambled around the corner of the whorehouse and headed alongside of it toward the street where he'd tied his horse so very long ago.

He was thinking in terms of the ride back to Good Enough and the cot that was waiting for him there.

He definitely was not thinking about pretty women who might be lurking in the shadows.

Not even when he walked right into the back of one and sent her sprawling plumb off her feet.

She had been standing in the shadows at a front corner of the whorehouse, and Longarm walked right into her when he came out from beside the building on his way to the street.

The woman went down in a flurry of flying skirts and startled yelps. She hit the ground face first, and some small object went skittering out of her hand.

Longarm recoiled in surprise but quickly knelt beside her in concern. She had taken a pretty hard tumble. "Are you all right, miss? I didn't . . . I mean t' say that I never . . ."

She spat a stream of Spanish at him that turned his ears red. And that was without him being able to understand a damn thing she was saying, she spoke so quickly. If he'd been able to make out all the words, no doubt she would've scorched his cheeks and turned his mustache to ashes.

"Carlotta? Is that you, Carlotta?"

"Sí, is . . . Señor Long? Is you, Señor Long? Aiii." She was off and running in Spanish again. But this time it didn't sound like anything a man would be afraid of listening to. She allowed him to help her up and to stand there fidgeting while she brushed herself off.

Longarm apologized profusely. And repeatedly. He hoped she was able to understand what he was saying. But surely she did. At least she seemed to be calming down after the unexpected assault from behind. No wonder she'd been scared, standing there minding her own business and the next thing she knows some idiot crashes into her from behind

107

and knocks her wig-over-wiggle. Anybody'd be upset by a thing like that.

Although what in hell an employee in the Sherman household would've been doing standing in the shadows outside a whorehouse at this time of night—shit, at any time of day or night—well, Longarm was a far piece from being able to figure that out.

He apologized again and then a few times more and figured he'd best do something constructive for a change so he probed around with the toe of his boot until he encountered something on the ground in the neighborhood of where Carlotta had dropped whatever thing it was she'd been holding.

When he picked it up, though, he was more confused than ever. He felt it. Then looked at it to confirm what it was he was holding. And finally he gave it back to her.

The tiny object Carlotta dropped when Longarm pounded her was a muff gun, one of those crazy-shaped little palm guns with a pancake cylinder and a pipsqueak rimfire caliber and a barrel not more than an inch long so nobody would ever have any notion which way a bullet out of it might want to travel. The things were mostly good for making noise and frightening would-be robbers away. Just right for a woman to protect herself with, but . . .

Dammit, what it came down to was that Carlotta, who should've been at home in bed up in that huge house up on top of the bluff, instead had been standing around at night down here. In front of a whorehouse. With a gun in her hand. Now that was what Longarm considered t' be mighty curious. He raised an eyebrow and waited for the girl to explain.

"I 'ave been waiting, señor. For you. To . . . you know . . . finish?" She sent a look in the direction of the whorehouse windows. By chance, George Freeman chose that particular moment to begin a loud and raucous reel. The sound of the piano was clear through the closed and drape-hung windows. "You horse, señor, it is there. I did not wan' to, you know, to go to the door an' ask for you. So I wait, eh? An' now," she shrugged and grinned, "now I 'ave foun' you."

Longarm found himself wanting to apologize all over again. The horse had been tied at the rail on the street there for quite a long time. He just hadn't bothered to move it with him when he went prowling through the saloons looking for Charley Hamer. So it was perfectly reasonable that Carlotta would have mistakenly thought he was inside Edna's drinking and rutting for all this time. And perfectly reasonable as well that she would be frightened enough to be hanging onto a muff gun while she hid and waited. Hell, an innocent girl, particularly one as pretty as Carlotta, wouldn't be safe from a bunch of drunks passing in and out of a place like Edna's. So of *course* she'd done exactly what she did here. Longarm couldn't blame her a bit.

Couldn't exactly come right out and tell her that he hadn't been getting himself laid either. That wasn't the sort of subject a man discussed with a woman unless he knew the woman awful well. What it was, he was just gonna have to let Carlotta assume whatever she pleased on that subject.

He mumbled another apology or two and finally got around to asking what it was she'd been wanting of him.

Carlotta looked flustered for a moment. Then she giggled. "I 'ave been so frighten, señor, that for a minute there I forget. My master, he want to know if there is more he can do for you. If anything you need, hmm? He send me to ask. But it is not so late when he send me, no? I think I 'ave stay here too long, but I was so scare I just stand an' shake. Now it is late, yes? Now I mus' go home. I . . . is anything I should tell my master, señor? You need anything from heem?"

"No. Nothing. Tell her thank you, but no."

Carlotta nodded and started away.

"Wait," Longarm said. "You were right. It is late. I can't let you go home by yourself, Carlotta."

"There is no need for that, señor."

"Nonsense. There is every need for that." He smiled. "If I let you go alone and anything happened to you, Carlotta, I could never forgive myself. Of course I'll see you safely home."

He couldn't help but notice once again just how awfully pretty this girl was. Not that that had anything to do with his offer to escort her back to The Folly. It really didn't.

109

But if there should be any opportunity for him to correct the girl's bad impressions of him, well . . . He gave her his most charming smile and offered his arm for her to take.

# Chapter 27

It was late by the time Longarm got Carlotta home. Almost too late, for Longarm's comfort, that is. The girl had walked down the path from The Folly to town. Naturally Longarm couldn't expect her to walk back up while he rode. Nor was he particularly inclined to let her ride while he walked. The logical solution was for the two of them to ride double. Logical, simple, effective.

And so damned uncomfortable that Custis Long was gritting his teeth and wanting to groan right out loud by the time they finally got to the back door of the big house atop the bluff.

Oh, the ride itself hadn't been uncomfortable. The Remount horse was as easy-gaited with two on his back as with one.

It was just that . . . well . . . it'd been too damned long by now since Longarm had had a warm female to snuggle up with. And poke into. And Carlotta was one helluva pretty girl. Built great. Soft, soft skin. Tiny wee waist. Dammit, she even smelled good.

She rode in front of Longarm, sharing a much too small space with him, so that she was rubbing all over the front of him while his arms had to be around her to reach the reins and . . . the upshot of the whole thing was that he was plain damned miserable.

And Carlotta, she seemed impervious to it all. She chattered a bit, mostly in Spanish, and unconsciously rubbed herself all over him with each and every movement of the lousy damned horse.

Before they'd ever hit the edge of Cimarron City it was a

wonder she couldn't feel the erection that was threatening to pop the buttons off Longarm's trousers. By the time they got to the top of the bluff the wonder was that Longarm hadn't come in his drawers. The girl had the softest, most gently enveloping ass . . . but she didn't feel a thing. Or anyway pretended that she didn't, which was the same thing. The point was that either Carlotta was uninterested in men and therefore was paying no attention to the stiff thing that was laid against her backside while they rode or she was uninterested in this particular man and therefore wanted to act like she had no notion of the effect she was causing behind her.

Much more of this, though, and Longarm was gonna have to stop at Edna's one more time tonight and pay for a piece of ass. He was getting that damn horny from the enforced but unreciprocated contact with Carlotta. By now the thought of a lonely army cot held no allure whatsoever.

"Whoa, boy, whoa. Steady. I'll get down first, Carlotta, then help you down," he said when finally he drew rein at the back of The Folly. He stepped out of the saddle and held himself turned half away so she wouldn't have to face the front of his pants sticking straight out at her when she was on the ground. He helped Carlotta off the horse. By that time the course of natural events had eliminated the problem and he was able to stand upright again without giving offense.

"You don' have to walk me to the door, señor," she said.

"I don't have to, no, but it'd be my pleasure," he smiled and lied. He offered the girl his elbow and escorted her the last few paces and up the steps to the back door.

Lights showed from several windows at the back of the house including at the kitchen where the back stoop and door were. The door was flung open almost instantly after Longarm's boots thumped on the boards of the steps, and a worried-looking Willard Sherman hurried out.

"Carlotta? Are you all right, my dear? And Long. Whatever are you doing here, man? Is she in trouble? Have you done something wrong, Carlotta? Where have you *been* all this time?" The questions came out all in a jumble, and the colonel, who was in his shirtsleeves and stocking feet, didn't

112

wait for answers before he spilled the next anxious query.

"Calm down, Colonel. Carlotta is just fine. And she's in no trouble. I'm only here t' make sure she got home safe."

"Thank you for that. But Carlotta. Wherever have you been, dear?"

The girl sent a nervous glance in Longarm's direction first and then another in Sherman's. She spoke rapidly in Spanish, her demeanor full of blushing apology. Sherman heard her out. Longarm couldn't tell what was being said, but the colonel's reactions were plain enough. At first there was the relief of knowing that the girl was all right. Then some irritation. Relief again. Finally some amusement. Eventually he laughed and took Carlotta by the elbow, drawing her inside the kitchen and motioning for Longarm to join them. There was no sign of Victoria Sherman inside at this hour nor of her father, but the other Mexican girl was there and there were two coffee cups on the table showing that both the servant and the master of the house had been sitting up waiting for Carlotta.

"Coffee, Long? Serena and I are floating in it. Been sitting here worrying for ever so long, you see. But now I understand. Carlotta misunderstood me when I mentioned wondering if there was anything else we might do for you. But then I believe I said it in English, which was my mistake. She doesn't understand all the nuances of our language, you see. I should have spoken in Spanish. As it is, somehow my simple comment was taken as an instruction. Although I would never, I assure you, send one of these girls off into town at night. Particularly not into the, um, rowdier districts. I shudder to think what might have happened to the child. If anything had, I could never have faced her father again. Thank you for seeing her safely home. Thank you."

There was no question that Sherman had been genuinely concerned about Carlotta. The man's relief now was as strong as his worry must have been. While Sherman was talking the other girl—Serena, he'd called her—was busy preparing a plate of small sandwiches and pickles. She set them in front of Longarm while the colonel eased him onto a chair at the table, and Carlotta meanwhile was pouring coffee for him.

"I didn't come here expecting t' be fed again," Longarm protested.

"Nonsense, man. It is all here. Why waste it? Besides, we owe you a debt of gratitude for bringing our Carlotta home. Please. Eat. Enjoy." Sherman smiled and motioned for the girls to fetch more plates. They did, distributing plates to everyone and then bringing out more food to pile onto the table. Leftover pies and cakes and cookies, homemade candies and sugared fruits—someone in the household certainly enjoyed sweets—and tidbits of cold meats, soft biscuits, hard rolls.

"Would you like Serena to fry you some potatoes to go with that, Long? Or some eggs? How about some ham then?" Sherman smiled and had a cookie.

"I'm fine. Honestly. Please don't go t' any trouble. I'm not at all hungry. Really."

It was all Longarm could do to get out of there without eating a full dinner. As it was he did stay long enough to have some coffee and a slice of pie—peach, he was always a sucker for peach pie—but managed to resist Sherman's entreaties that he stay the night.

"We have more than enough room, and you would be most welcome, I assure you," the colonel insisted.

"That's mighty kind o' you, but I'll pass. Thanks." The truth was that Longarm would've been happy for an excuse to stay if he'd gotten any come-ahead signals from Carlotta on the way up. Or, hell, from Serena now. He was horny enough at the moment to give serious thought to jumping a nanny goat if he could get somebody to bathe and perfume the critter. But with neither girl seeming interested, well, it'd be pushing the limits of endurance to sleep so near and not be able to touch. "Mighty nice of you, sir. I appreciate it." He smiled and stood and wiped his mouth with his napkin. "If you would excuse me now, I'll be on m' way."

"If you must."

"Yes, sir. Reckon I must."

"Then I bid you thanks and good night, Longarm."

By the time Longarm reached the bay horse the lamps in the kitchen had been extinguished, and the back of the

114

Sherman house was in darkness.

Longarm burped and stood beside the bay's shoulder while he pulled a cheroot from his coat and lighted it. It was going to be a long, lonely ride back to Good Enough.

# Chapter 28

Movement off to the right caught Longarm's eye. Furtive movement, he thought. He glimpsed it and then it was withdrawn. Without being obvious about it he looked more closely. There was a carriage house over there where he'd just seen something moving. More shed than house, really, with a roof and three walls but the front left open. The tongues of two wagon rigs were visible in the shadows.

Something—he wasn't at all sure what—had just been moving inside the shed. Now . . . nothing.

That might not have bothered him so much as a normal run of things. He was on another man's property and there was no telling how many employees Willard Sherman had nor what they might be up to at any given hour of the day. Or night.

But just a little while ago Harry Shelton had tried to put a slug into Longarm's belly. That sort of thing just naturally tended to make a man walk shy of shadows and of folks in hiding. After all, there'd been time enough for Harry to follow Longarm and Carlotta up the path and take up ambush in that shed over there.

Longarm cleared his throat and drew deep on the cheroot he'd just lighted. Striking a match out in the open like that had made him a better target than he'd given thought to. Luckily enough, the bay horse was standing between him and the carriage shed. In a deal like that a halfway sensible ambusher wouldn't risk a shot until the victim stepped up into his saddle and made a better target of himself.

If there was an ambusher, that is. Whoever was in that shed might just be some cowboy or vaquero come to strum a tune under Serena's bedroom window and be shy about being caught at it by a stranger.

But, dammit, whoever was in that shed could also be Harry Shelton with a gun in his hand.

Longarm didn't feel much inclined to crawl up atop that saddle and take a chance on which the answer turned out to be. Because guessing wrong could be a whole lot more uncomfortable than mere embarrassment.

He took another deep drag on the cigar and then with a loud grunt "accidentally" dropped it to the ground.

When he bent as if to retrieve the cheroot he was hidden behind the body of the horse. He spun and dropped into a crouch before darting away at an angle that quickly carried him to the side of the carriage shed. Anyone inside the three-sided structure would be left now with a view of The Folly and of Longarm's horse. But not much else.

Longarm cat-footed up beside the carriage shed and leaned against the wall. He concentrated on listening, knowing that even folks who should know better tend to get hung up on looking for danger when at night it is a man's ears that are by far the more likely to protect him than his eyes.

Almost immediately he heard the muted creak of steel springs as one of the wagons rocked slightly on its running gear. Whoever was inside that carriage house—and there was no question now that somebody damn sure was—was in or on one of the wagons.

The sound of the springs moving was repeated, louder this time. As if the person were getting down to ground level. Longarm's expression turned grim.

Someone was in there just a few feet away from him on the other side of a flimsy wall. Whoever it was had seen him come out of the Sherman house and light that cigar, had seen him disappear, had to know that now the tall deputy marshal was loose in the night and wondering what in hell was going on here.

Given all that, Longarm figured, any innocent swain come to pay court to one of the colonel's hired girls would surely be wanting to speak up and announce himself lest gunplay commence.

Yet there was only silence from inside the shed.

Which sure as hell hinted that the person inside there had no good intentions.

Longarm eased the big Colt out of his holster and held it at the ready while he crept along the wall toward the front of the shed, stopping only when he had reached the end of the wall.

He could burst around into plain sight, of course. And silhouette himself as a target for anyone inside.

Or he could conclude to wait the guy out, standing here all damn night if necessary until daybreak and the sun-facing open front of the shed promised to blind anyone standing inside and looking out. That would effectively switch the odds around and put things into Longarm's favor.

Or he could opt for neither of those. And it seemed like he wouldn't have to. He was sure he could hear breathing now. Someone was standing so close that he could almost feel their body heat seeping around the end of the shed wall. Whoever was inside that shed was standing immediately beside Longarm except for the width of the wall boards. He could feel that. Could actually smell soap on the guy.

Longarm frowned. And silently sniffed. It was soap, all right. He could smell it plain. The guy was freshly bathed. And hadn't been drinking. Whoever it was—not Harry Shelton—didn't smell of liquor at all. But if he wasn't Harry, and wasn't wanting to announce himself to Longarm, who the hell was this and what was he doing here in the middle of the night. Someone else wanting to ambush a deputy United States marshal? Somebody wanting to do harm to the Sherman family?

There was a good way to find out.

Longarm returned the Colt to its holster—this wasn't Shelton and as yet there was no reason to turn lethal here—and braced himself ready to swing around the end of the wall and tackle whoever was standing so close inside there.

On the count of three, he mentally prompted, tensing his muscles and coiling like a snake ready to strike. One . . . two . . .

# Chapter 29

It was kinda like tackling a pale bit of curtain fabric that was billowing at an open window on a breezy day.

Kinda like that. Or maybe like making an ass of oneself.

Longarm whirled around the end wall of that carriage shed and launched himself shoulder first, and hard, into the midsection of a tiny wee human being.

The two of them weren't halfway to the ground before Longarm realized he'd just gone and flung himself on top of the colonel's lady.

Who of course had every right t' be sitting in her own carriage shed in the middle of the night.

And who no-damned-wonder wouldn't want t' be seen by some idiot stranger while she was doing it because what she happened t' be wearing at the moment—as Longarm could plainly tell because he had his nose pushed into folds upon folds of the sheer, gauzy stuff—was a filmy, flimsy, fancy sort of nightdress.

He clutched at the woman and rolled with her, trying to get over sideways so he could break her fall. Instead of falling onto her and breaking *her*, that is.

He was only partially successful. He landed as much beside her as on her. Unfortunately the part of him that was lying on her came down hard and square in the belly.

Victoria Sherman might have cried out except that she hadn't any breath left to do it with. Longarm heard all the air whooshing out of her with a grunt.

"Oh, shit," he muttered as he scrambled to all fours and made a grab trying to pull her upright again. What he was thinking of with that maneuver he honestly couldn't have explained. For sure it wasn't that he expected she wouldn't notice any of it happened if he got her back onto her feet quick enough.

Whatever he had in mind, though, it didn't work.

Instead of grabbing the lady's hand and snatching her upright he ended up grabbing her left tit. And squeezing it. Hard. But not hard enough that he could take a good hold and haul her to her feet by it. Thank goodness for small favors.

Longarm yelped. Victoria Sherman did too. He was pretty sure they were yipping for two entirely different reasons. His was alarm. Apology. Stuff like that. Hers was more likely to've been out of sheer pain. After all, he'd just about ripped her left one plumb off.

"Oh, jeez," he groaned. "Oh, shit, what've I gone an' done now."

Mrs. Sherman's slight body—she wasn't hardly big enough to be keeping size—was convulsing and shuddering and kind of jumping around.

"Calm down, ma'am. I . . . if you can force yourself t' be still for just a minute there an' get your breath back you'll be able t' yell for help. An' I won't blame you neither. Lordy, I can just imagine what you must think I was trying t' do just then. You . . . naw, you prob'ly don't want me helping you up. Better I get back an' leave be, huh?"

Mrs. Sherman sputtered and bounced and thumped her palms hard against the ground. She was laying back in the dirt now and wallowing around, thrashing her head from side to side and drumming her feet.

Longarm felt mortified. He must've gone and scared the poor woman into a fit of some kind. A convulsion. Maybe even a heart attack. If she went and died from this treatment . . .

He didn't know what a body was supposed to do in a situation like this but he recognized that something had to be done to save the poor woman's life. And done damned quick too.

He jumped to her side—careful this time to not to plant a knee in her belly or something—and took her by the shoulders.

"Ma'am? Miz Sherman? What can I do for you, ma'am? Here, ma'am, be careful you don't bite your tongue. You'll choke t' death if you swallow your tongue. Let me get ahold here." He grabbed her jaw and tried to hold it open so he could work a hand inside her mouth and secure her tongue. That was dangerous, he knew. A person could get bit that way, bit awful bad, and there isn't much that's worse for festering than a human bite. Never mind that, though. He owed this little woman. If she went and died here it would be all his fault. He pulled and twisted at her jaw to force it open and then reached inside.

Mrs. Sherman resisted at first, then gave in as she seemed to realize what he was trying to do. He probed inside her mouth to find her tongue. It was a slippery damn thing, though. Kept sliding out of his grasp whenever he tried to hold it.

"Be easy now, easy," he crooned, that and stuff of that nature, over and over softly the way a body will do when he's trying to soothe and gentle a frightened colt.

After a bit it occurred to him that Mrs. Sherman wasn't thrashing around any longer. She was just kind of laying on the ground there with Longarm's fist stuffed halfway down her throat. "Ma'am? Are you all right now, ma'am?"

Her only response was an attempt to nod. Which, everything considered, was about all she was capable of doing. Longarm recognized the problem and withdrew his hand from the lady's mouth.

Mrs. Sherman—incredibly—immediately resumed her convulsions. Except this time he could tell that what she was doing was laughing. Laughing t' beat all bill hell, in fact.

"Ma'am?"

"M-m-m-m . . ." She gave up trying to form the word and yelped with laughter, clutching at her belly with one hand and pounding on the dirt with the other. "Y-y-y-you . . ." That was the best she could manage for the moment. She thrashed her head from side to side and beat on the earth and shrieked with laughter, obviously trying to mute the noise she was making but not doing a very good job of it.

Longarm felt more foolish than ever. It'd been bad enough when he thought he'd gone and killed her. In a way this was even worse. He felt his ears turn hot and realized it was a damn good thing the interior of this shed was so dark. "I reckon you're all right after all," he drawled. He pulled back away from the nearly hysterical woman and sat cross-legged on the dirt floor. His first cheroot was laying on the ground somewhere out by the horse so he pulled out another and lighted it while the woman's guffaws subsided into mere giggles.

"I only did that, y' understand, so's to amuse you," he ventured after a bit. Which set her off again, but more briefly this time.

"Please don't make me laugh any more. My stomach already hurts from it." She held a hand out to him. For a change he comprehended what was happening and took hold of it, pulling her up into a sitting position. The two of them ended up seated knee to knee on the hard soil of the carriage shed floor.

"I didn't hurt you bad?"

"No." She giggled a few times more. "You certainly did startle me out of my wits."

"Huh. You weren't the only one got a surprise."

"Would you mind telling me what you were trying to do, sir?"

He explained. He certainly owed her that much.

"I see. Well, Marshal, I must say I am glad the truth was not so dramatic."

"Longarm," he corrected her.

"Then you shall call me Victoria, please."

"Sure."

"You really were quite a sight, Longarm. Springing out of nowhere like that. Bearing me down with you. But so quick and strong. Why, for anyone to be able to twist like that without warning and keep me from being hurt. I was impressed."

"Time I realized what I'd gone and done, ma'am . . ."

"Victoria," she said.

"Right. Victoria. Time I realized . . ."

"You are dreadfully strong, aren't you?" she said. And this time there was no laughter in her voice.

Victoria Sherman, the colonel's grand lady, leaned forward, the front of her nightdress falling open a bit, and gave Longarm's bicep a slow, gentle squeeze that was more caress than anything else.

He cleared his throat. "I kinda get the impression you aren't in a hurry t' get back inside now?"

She smiled and tilted her head to the side. For such a plain little woman she was an almighty attractive one somehow.

Longarm sure as hell understood what was going on here. He couldn't make any sense out of why it was happening.

But it was damn sure happening.

Never one to kick gift horses in the butt, Longarm reached out. Victoria came into his arms and lifted her face to his. Her own arms slid warm and eager around him, and the colonel's wife pressed herself hot and willing to Longarm's hard body.

# Chapter 30

Victoria had something of an advantage over him. She was already virtually undressed. A quick sweep of her arms sent the nightdress over her head and away, and she was naked before him.

Longarm found himself wishing for more moonlight so he could better see and appreciate what he was being given here.

Victoria Sherman was small, but she was a mouthful. Her waist was impossibly narrow and her hips a delightful hourglass shape despite their diminutive size.

Her breasts, although not large, were hard and distended, with prominent nipples and a perky, jutting shape. Longarm hadn't remembered why that would be so until Victoria knelt in front of his seated figure, raising herself so that her left breast, the one he had so cruelly squeezed, was brushing lightly against his lips.

In a situation like that just what is a fella supposed to do, anyway. Longarm did what nature demanded and pulled her nipple into his mouth, gently rolling it on his tongue and sucking it.

Victoria's body temperature was the same as his so that it took him a moment to realize that the flavor of her was not the flavor of her skin but of the bland, warm milk that was flowing from her breast into his mouth.

But then the lady's husband had mentioned something about her nursing a baby girl. It was a fact that hadn't especially registered with Longarm. Then. Now was quite another story.

"Nice," Victoria whispered. "No, don't pull away. More, please. Now this one."

With a coyly playful smile Victoria pulled back from him a few inches and turned so that her right breast was to him. She took hold of herself and squeezed, sending a miniature stream of warm milk into Longarm's mouth in much the same way a farmer can direct milk from an udder to a waiting kitten. Or in this case, tomcat.

"So nice," she repeated as she pressed her nipple to his lips. He drank from her body, not nearly as excited by the process as Victoria seemed to be but certainly finding no objection to this exercise in pleasing her. "Hard. Hard now, Longarm. Yes."

After a few more moments she reluctantly drew away from him and dropped down onto her heels. "I have to save some. Gloria will need her night feeding in another hour or so."

Longarm assumed that Gloria was the baby but didn't ask. Odd as Victoria was acting at the moment it could also turn out that Gloria was a servant girl. And if that was the case Longarm would rather not know anyhow.

Victoria smiled and helped Longarm with his buttons. When he too was naked she pressed her face against his chest and teasingly suckled his nipples much as she had demanded that he suckle hers. Albeit with somewhat less result than he had obtained. She did not seem to mind that difference.

"Wait a moment, dear," she said. She stood and reached into the body of the light surrey they were beside. She brought a lap robe out and spread it on the ground for their comfort. Longarm moved onto the robe and Victoria joined him.

"You're glorious," she whispered as she stroked him with both hands. "So beautiful. I want everything. Do you mind? I want to feel this beautiful thing inside me, but I want to taste it too. It's been so long since I've tasted a man's flesh. Would you mind that?"

"I'll try an' put up with it," he promised.

Victoria chuckled and knelt at his side. Her hair was unpinned. It cascaded over his cock and his balls like a

125

silken tent of pleasure as she bent to him, holding herself poised above him for a moment while she drew in several long breaths. It took him a moment before he realized that what the woman was doing was smelling of him. He didn't mind. While she was doing that her exhalations were laving him in warm air, tantalizing and teasing and building him all that much higher. As if he needed any more building.

Finally she nipped and nibbled at the head of his cock, running her lips up and down the shaft, touching him with gentle fingertips, lightly tasting and teasing before she parted her lips and lowered her head onto him.

He felt the warmth of her engulf him, surrounding and capturing him. Her tongue was wet and hot on him, and her mouth and throat were tight around him. Longarm groaned softly and lifted his hips to meet her.

Victoria gurgled something that might have been a sound of happy agreement and cupped his balls in the palm of her hand, stroking and squeezing and toying with him there while she suckled his pecker. The combination of sensations was so intense that it sent small jolts and shivers of feeling through his belly and down both his legs.

Victoria withdrew from him. "You drank from me, dear, and I want to drink from you. But I want to feel you inside me too. It's been so *long,* you see. Too long. Like I said, I want it all."

"We in a hurry?"

"No."

"Then you do whatever you want, honey. Late as it is I don't reckon you can wear me out before dawn, so just you have at it an' do whatever pleases."

"You can do it more than once?"

"Hell yes." Victoria grinned gleefully. It occurred to Longarm to wonder just what was wrong with Willard Sherman if the fella never romped this eager young woman more than just once in a night. But that was hardly the sort of question he was likely to ask at a time like this.

Victoria's response was to shower his prick with kisses of joy. Kisses that turned quickly into something considerably more serious as she once again took him deep into her mouth. But this time with the clear intent to do more than simply tantalize.

Longarm figured under the circumstances—and hell, he knew she'd just bathed; soap was what he'd been able to smell on her before he even knew it was her on the far side of that wall—it was only fair for him to return the favor.

While Victoria's pale and slender neck remained impaled on his playful spear, Longarm pulled her around so that she lay on top of him, her belly pressed against his chest and her mouth still wrapped tight around his cock. He pulled her legs apart and arranged her thighs against his ears—damned handy muffs if the night decided to turn cold; a fella couldn't ever be too careful of such worries—and nuzzled into the slippery wet folds that were conveniently positioned over his chin.

"What are you doing?" Victoria asked, releasing him for the moment.

"Y' mean you don't know?"

"No."

"Boy, are you in for a s'prise." His tongue flicked, and Victoria jumped like she'd just been poked with a sharp object. Then she groaned and wriggled her hips. From the way she acted he suspected that what she was feeling was somewhat better than a sharp jab.

"Now I am glad that you," she giggled, "ran into me." With a sigh and a wiggle Victoria lowered herself at both ends, one to make things easier for Longarm. And the other shoving him so deep inside her throat that it was a wonder she didn't gag. Somehow, though, she was able to accommodate all of him, swallowing his cock until the point of her chin was poking hard into his lower belly. Then she began rocking back and forth, moving a scant fraction of an inch at a time so that the sensations were slow and subtle. But almighty damned insistent.

When finally he couldn't stand it any longer and began a long, slow flow of come from his balls to her belly, Victoria stayed right where she was, still suckling and pulling and using her hands on his balls to encourage him. He had first drunk of her fluids and now she drank of his.

The exchange, Longarm figured, seemed entirely fair.

And then it was her turn, Victoria proving to be as willing a student as she was a performer.

Later, though, when they were both sitting upright again and Longarm had relighted his neglected smoke, Victoria lay her head on his shoulder and sighed. "If you were leading me on so that you could come in my mouth, dear, I'll forgive you. I really won't mind."

"You mean about being able t' make it more'n just the once?"

"Uh huh." She turned her head and kissed his chest.

Longarm chuckled and took her hand, placing it into his lap where already he was commencing to lengthen and turn hard again in anticipation of seconds.

Victoria's eyes went wide. And then she smiled. She kissed him with a fierce intensity, then lay back on the robe and pulled at him in mute request that he mount her.

Longarm figured he didn't have to be in all that big a hurry to finish this cheroot. After all, he could relight it one more time.

He stretched out beside her, and Victoria opened herself, tugging and demanding with an eager, innocent abandon until he raised himself over her supine body and plunged himself deep into her receptive flesh.

Small though she was there was a deceptive strength in this colonel's lady, and she was a woman who was willing to give back every bit as good as she got.

All Longarm had to do was dig in his spurs—figuratively speaking, that is—and hang on for a wild and wonderful ride.

"Ride 'em, cowboy," he muttered.

"What, dear?"

"Nothin'."

"Then hush. I can already feel this one starting. Down there around my toes. I can feel them curling, dear. Oh. Oh, goodness. *Oh!*" Her fingernails dug into his back like she was trying to bury them there, but he didn't mind. Not right then he didn't. He just hung on and let 'er buck.

# Chapter 31

Longarm sighed, yawned once, and then drew deep on the cheroot. It seemed he was finally going to get to enjoy that smoke after all. Not that he minded the several delays that had brought him to this point, of course. It was just that he liked a good cigar too.

Victoria snuggled tight against his side. She seemed as content, and as thoroughly sated, as Longarm felt. Longarm swore he could almost hear her purring. The two of them were seated on the now rather rumpled and sweaty blanket and were leaning against the spokes of the surrey's left hind wheel. Victoria picked up Longarm's discarded tweed coat and draped it over herself against the cool of the evening air. He knew for certain that that was what she had in mind because this girl damn sure wasn't one for modesty. He just hoped she didn't dribble any milk onto the liner of his coat. Her tits had begun to leak lately, so it was probably time for her to go in and give the baby a nursing.

"You must think I'm a terrible hussy," Victoria said.

"Nonsense." Longarm knew enough about women by now to realize that a question like that has nothing to do with any expectation that the man could actually believe anything the woman might be accusing herself of. It really means that she wants a compliment. And likely something more to head off any need for her to feel guilty about having strayed outside her own pasture. "You are a bright an' beautiful woman, Victoria. I'm just mighty proud you care enough 'bout me to share your charming self with me. Being with you has been special, real special. I count myself lucky," he added, without having to think about what he was saying. It was the sort of shit that a man learns to parrot at whatever moments seem appropriate, like reciting a poem learned by rote so that the fella saying it never again has to listen to the words or think about the meaning of what he's spouting. He concluded with a smiling thank you and a light kiss planted on her temple. What he was really thinking about, though, was how much he was enjoying his cheroot now that he finally had it afire and a few minutes of peace and privacy to smoke on it.

Victoria sighed loudly and tucked herself all that much closer to him. She laid her cheek against his chest and wrapped both her arms about him. "I know I should feel shameless and awful," she said, "but I don't. Right now I'm much too happy to feel anything but good, dear. You make me feel so . . . alive. So wanted. And it had been so awfully long since . . . I mean, with only Da and my husband on the ranch, and Willard and I never . . . that is to say . . . oh, I . . . please don't pay any mind to me, dear. I've gotten wound up and now I'm being silly. Sometimes I can be such a goose. Please forget I said anything."

"Anything you ask, dear lady, will be my pleasure t' give." That too was by rote. The simple truth was that Longarm did not really give a fat crap how often Willard and Victoria Sherman bumped bellies. And if for some reason they didn't do the dirty deed any longer—because of the kid, say, or for whatever other reason—it was neither any of Longarm's business nor any point of tiny interest to him. Victoria had chosen of her own free will to crawl his cock. He hadn't asked her much less forced her to it. But once it was freely offered he hadn't seen any reason to push her away and saw no reason now to either question or condemn her for it. And if she wanted to make the same offer some other time, why, Custis Long was almost sure to respond the very same way then too. But in the meanwhile he saw no reason to offer up explanations or apologies nor to pick it all apart with analysis and justifications.

Victoria sighed again and hugged him. "You are so good, Longarm. You make me feel so warm and wanted. I had

130

forgotten how nice it can be to be with a man."

Longarm thought that sounded like she was gilding the lily a mite. But what the hell. He mumbled a few more comforting phrases without bothering to listen to which ones he was telling her this time.

"Will I see you again, dear?" she asked, this time with a note of worry in her voice.

"D'you want to?" he asked. A guy never knew. Some women like to have their fun but then afterward want to pretend they never did. Others make the mistake of thinking that pussy juice is a kind of glue that binds a man to them forever and ever more.

"Yes," Victoria said with a simple, heartfelt sincerity that was unmistakable. "If you want to. Any time you want to. Call out to me, dear, and I'll come to you even if I have to crawl on my knees." She kissed his chest and neck and hugged him with a sudden, fierce strength. It occurred to him that her breath had turned hot all of a sudden and her shoulders were gently shuddering; she'd begun to cry from the intensity of the offer she was making.

"You ain't thinking . . . I mean . . . ?" He wasn't sure just how to put this without being insulting.

"Don't worry, dear. I'm not turning possessive of you. Even if I wanted to, I . . . but never mind about that." She looked up at him with a smile. "All I want of you, dear, is the pleasure of having you hold me." The smile turned into a grin. "And having you do things to me, of course. You know the things I mean." She wriggled her hips and chuckled.

"Every chance I get," he promised. And this time he was not speaking by rote. Victoria was a joy to fuck, eager and inventive and game for anything either one of them could think up.

"Good!" she declared happily. "Um, you wouldn't just one more time want to, uh . . ." She took hold of him and squeezed suggestively.

A few minutes earlier Longarm had been quite sure he was used up and useless until he'd had time to get some serious rest. Now he wasn't so sure about that. And by now he'd had time to enjoy all the smoking he really needed for the time being. Why it was just possible after all that he might. . . .

"Señora?" Serena appeared in the open mouth of the shed without a sound. She was barefoot on the sunbaked earth and had made no noise when she approached.

Longarm froze in place. Yet—funny—he felt Victoria jump from being startled but after that felt no tension whatsoever in the woman's slim and vibrant little body. It didn't seem to bother her a whole lot that she'd been found in the arms of a man who wasn't her husband.

"Yes, Serena?"

"The babe, señora, she is fretful. She needs the milk now, sí?"

"Sí, Serena. Thank you."

The servant girl stood there quite certainly able to see and comprehend the tableau at her feet—a naked couple and a blanket spread out on the ground weren't what you might call mysterious as to intent—and never so much as blinked. She just stood there and looked at them like this was the most natural thing there could be in a carriage shed in the middle o' the damn night.

Victoria let go of Longarm's cock and kissed him, then held a hand up to Serena. The Mexican girl helped Victoria to her feet and handed the woman the long ago discarded nightdress.

Longarm noted with some amusement that Serena daintily, and rather surreptitiously, wiped the palm of her hand on her skirt. But then Victoria had been playing with Longarm's pecker, and that much-used device was sticky with the drying residues of an awful lot of vigorous screwing. No doubt some of it'd gotten onto Serena when she helped Victoria to her feet.

Longarm stood up—it was too late now to be worrying about modesty—and bent to receive the good night kiss Victoria offered.

Then the two women went off together toward the house.

Longarm grunted softly to himself, not at all sure how he oughta take these last couple minutes, then retrieved his clothes and began to dress.

The bay horse was still waiting patiently near the back door of The Folly. Longarm wasn't sure of the time but he suspected he would make it back to Good Enough just about in time for breakfast now.

The loss of those few hours of sleep, he figured, hadn't been any hardship whatsoever.

# Chapter 32

It was actually later than Longarm realized. By the time he was halfway down the steep, switchback path that led from The Folly down to the floor of Big Skull Wash there was bright light spreading across the horizon out to the east where the dry and mostly empty plains rolled on for another thousand miles, give or take a stone's throw.

Staying up to play is one thing, but missing an entire night's sleep is another. Longarm hadn't known how tired he was until he saw the sun commencing to come up. Soon as he realized what time it was he was exhausted. Then about half a minute later he realized how dumb he was being on the subject and gave himself firm instructions to quit being so damn silly. It was only a few hours of sleep that he'd missed, after all. And for a helluva good cause.

What he really needed, he figured, was a cup of coffee and ten pounds or so of breakfast. Instead of cutting behind the town and loping straight out to the army post like he'd planned, he stayed on the path and into Cimarron City.

At this early hour there was a surprising amount of foot traffic on the streets and plenty of trade under way in the cafés as men by the dozens sauntered, bounced, or sometimes crept their way out in search of breakfast and those first, heart-starting cups of morning coffee. From the way some of these fellows looked Longarm figured he was right at home amongst them. In better shape than most, actually.

He tied the bay outside an exceptionally busy café at the edge of town, going on the theory that popularity comes from quality, and joined the collection of humanity that was standing in line there waiting for table space.

134

The folks who had arrived early enough to already have seats were mostly town-dressed. Longarm guessed them to be shopkeepers and store clerks and the like, on their way to work and following a routine that probably had them eating here at this same place most every morning of their workaday lives. That bunch looked well rested and wide awake, most of them fresh shaved already and acting chipper and cheerful enough to piss off anybody that wasn't feeling as bushy-tailed as they were.

This particular morning Longarm felt somewhat more at home among the fellows who had come later and were standing in line. They for the most part were rough-dressed with wide-brimmed hats and high-heeled boots. They were bleary-eyed and bewhiskered, wearing rumpled clothes from having slept in strange places, and they smelled of a blend of stale tobacco smoke, spilled beer, and cheap perfume. None of this bunch looked much more wide awake than Longarm was.

Longarm quick enough discovered what at least one of the draws was to this particular café. And a damned welcome one it was too. Double-barreled welcome, in fact.

A woman came outside carrying a coffeepot in one hand and a bucket in the other. Wisps of aromatic steam lifted out of the spout of the coffeepot. And the bucket was tumbled full of tin mugs. Seeing the lady work her way down the line of waiting customers handing out free cups of eye-opener coffee was a welcome thing indeed.

Seeing the lady by and of itself woulda been mighty welcome too if Longarm hadn't just left Victoria Sherman's vigorous embraces.

This woman was middle-aged but plenty handsome. She had streaks of gray running through her hair, but her figure was lush and full and her smile was the sort that can light up an entire room.

"Here y' go, hon. Help yourself to one of those cups. That's right. Don't crowd now, boys, there's plenty enough for all. If this pot runs dry I'll bring out another. Help yourself there, hon."

The men blinked and grinned and muttered. Most of them grabbed their hats with one hand and a coffee cup with the other when the lady reached them.

"Thankee, ma'am, you're an angel." "I think you done saved my life, missus." "Gee, thanks."

Good-looking though the woman was there wasn't a lewd look nor a bawdy remark passed, not to the woman directly and not behind her back afterward. But then anybody who ventured such a breach of civility likely would have been bloodied and battered some by way of an introduction to good manners. It had been Longarm's experience that most cowboys are sticklers for decent behavior among decent woman. And anybody who doesn't understand this to begin with will soon receive instruction on the subject.

"Thank you, ma'am, thank you," the man standing next to Longarm whispered with fervor. The fellow was so wobbly he couldn't steady his cup with less than two hands, but rather than wear his sombrero in front of this lady he dropped the thing on the ground so he could devote both hands to the serious business of holding onto that life-giving cup.

Longarm swept his own Stetson off a moment later and plucked a cup out of the bucket. "Thank you, ma'am."

The lady's smile—she had gray eyes, he noticed, and a velvety skin texture . . . and a wedding band on the ring finger of her right hand, which pretty much identified her as being married all right but coming from someplace in Europe—was just about as warming as the coffee. Lucky man, her husband.

"Whew!" the man beside Longarm said after he'd gulped his first few swallows. "That sure sets a man up, don't it?" All up and down the line, Longarm could see, the men were feeling more cheerful and talkative now.

Longarm took a swallow too. Then smacked his lips loudly. "Yeah, don't it," he said with a grin. This wasn't the sort of coffee that's brewed for pussies or pilgrims. This was coffee fit for a trail-droving camp. Hair-on-the-chest, spike-floating, takes-a-knife-to-cut-it *coffee*. Longarm smiled and had another swallow. Hell, he just might live after all.

"What outfit you with, neighbor?" the man beside him asked.

"Pardon?"

"I said . . ."

"Oh, right." Longarm yawned and apologized.

"That's all right, friend. I had me a fun night too." He winked.

"I'm not with an outfit," Longarm explained. "Just passing through." There wasn't any point in elaborating on the subject. "You?"

"The F R Connected. Up from West Texas."

"Lot o' you boys in town, I see," Longarm said. "I'm surprised there'd be so many herds coming through when we're so far below the Arkansas."

The cowboy snorted. "It ain't everybody comes through Kansas, y'know. Been lots o' buyers down our way from Wyoming, Montana, them places. Opening lotsa graze up there, I take it."

Longarm nodded. There was plenty of rich new grassland being opened to use as fewer and fewer Indian hostilities interfered with development.

"They're buying plenty of cattle out o' our country an' New Mexico too. All through the Pecos country, like. Stockers, mostly. Young cows especially. Not s' many bulls. They're mostly wantin' t' bring in their own bulls an' crossbreed, make them some stock that'll stand up t' the cold winters. Anyhow, at least for a while, mister, you'll find plenty o' cow herds moving outta our country an' up the road here." The cowboy snorted again. "From that direction a man damn near has t' come this way, like it or don't. Poor water t' the south o' here, but there's no quarantines against the ticks. And over east on the Indian land there's two ways t' find troubles. Raiding parties of young bucks that don't realize them days is supposed t' be over or a worse kind o' raiding party from the older, smarter Indians that do realize it an' have started raiding the trail herds by way o' trespass fees. So all in all it's easier for us t' come north along the Pecos Valley an' then up the old Cimarron Cut-off. Angle off o' that . . . the place is marked now . . . an' we come out onto the Ogallala Trail just below this town. Which we was mighty glad t' see, let me tell you. Wasn't none of us had a drink nor a woman nor any company but our own for better'n a month till we got here. But that wasn't what I was saying, was it. My point was, can't no son of a bitch charge us fees or block us out when we're on the Ogallala Road. Us and our cow herds is what the dang thing is here for, right?"

"Damn right," Longarm agreed. "Interesting what you said about being able to expect more trail herds through here."

"Long as them boys up in Wyoming an' Montana, Dakota Territory, all up through there, long as that country is bein' developed an' opening t' cattle there'll be herds o' stockers driving up from Texas an' New Mexico. Count on it. And we'll be comin' this way regular up till the railroad comes through an' we can ship instead o' drivin'. Maybe even after since it seems like they don't never build railroads up an' down but just east-west sidewards. Might still have t' use the ol' Ogallala. An' o' course the cows'll still have t' reach the rails no matter what else happens. I'll always have my work. Am I right, neighbor, or am I right?"

"You're right, all right." Longarm took a swallow of the coffee. "You've given all this some thought," he said.

"No need to. It's plain as a boil on your own butt what's happening." The fellow grinned again. He had roughly half his own teeth left. Which probably wasn't all that bad an average, everything considered. Bad horses and cranky cattle seem to conspire to deprive a man of his teeth. "Wonder if that nice lady is gonna come 'round with the pot again."

"I dunno, but I'd mention her in my will if I had anything worth leaving to her," another cowboy put in.

"Shit, Huey, you won't never have anything to leave to no lady."

Huey chuckled and scratched himself. "Maybe so, but I think a lady left me something last night."

"Lady?"

"Damn right Fat Helen is a lady. She made me take my boots off, didn't she?"

"Reckon that's as close as you or me will ever come, Huey," Longarm's talkative neighbor agreed. He laughed. "Them crabs o' yours is close as either of us will come t' having our own livestock too, eh?"

The two cowboys went to jawing at one another. Longarm rocked back on his heels—he suspected he was one of very few in this line who had balance enough to be able to do so right now—and polished off the last of the coffee.

He felt damn near human again after drinking it.

# Chapter 33

After breakfast Longarm left the horse tied where it was and ambled on into the business district. It still would have been considered early by Denver's standards, but here the working day was well under way. There was hardly a shop or a store that wasn't already open for business. Including the saloons, although those were among the less patronized places at this hour.

He found what he wanted easily enough, but again there was a line of customers waiting. Longarm lifted an eyebrow to the barber, who surveyed the crowd of cowboys already settled in to wait as long as required. "Hour and a half. Maybe a little longer," the barber said.

Longarm grunted and felt of the prickly beard stubble on his jaw. He needed a shave, no doubt about that. But he hated like hell to have to wait that long. "I'll be back," he said.

"Suit yourself, friend." The barber casually stroked the lathered cheek of the man who was already in his chair.

It never ceased to amaze Longarm how a good barber could handle a razor. Anybody try to shave himself with that same speed and confidence and he'd end up slicing flaps of meat off his cheek like he was filleting a trout. The barber in this shop was so good he could stroke and carve like he was using a butter knife instead of a hollow ground razor that likely could cut a hair in two lengthwise as easy as across. It was a skill Longarm admired.

Longarm watched a moment longer just for the pleasure of it, then started to turn away.

He paused before he ever stepped out in the direction of the door, though, and turned back again.

This time he was looking not at the barber but toward the floor.

The customer who was receiving his shave was a cowboy. Longarm could see that plain as plain could be even though the man was covered from knees to neck with the barber's cloth. The runover boots and fancy spurs gave him away. A man might not have room enough to pack Saturday night boots or a Sunday morning hat on the trail, but there's always space enough to tuck away a set of go-to-hell spurs. And most working hands set great store by their personal turnout. In a trail town it's usual for the visiting cowboys to ride in wearing spurs worth more than all the rest of their outfits combined, horse and saddle included. The bunch waiting in this barber shop was no different. And as at breakfast earlier, nearly all the customers at the moment were cowboys in off the Ogallala.

The sweat-crusted hats and manure-stained boots were worn together with spurs that were decorated with drooping peso rowels and chased silver carvings and brass ladylegs and even a few brightly polished jinglers, little bells that would tinkle and chime whenever the wearer took a step. Longarm suspected he was looking at the fruits of more jewelers' efforts here in this barber shop than could be found on the wrists and ears of the women at most big city soirees.

Cowboys. All of them cowboys.

He frowned, wondering why in hell that seemed so bothersome to him just now. Something somebody'd said. The cowboy he talked to before breakfast, that happy, shaking, friendly fellow up from West Texas? Maybe.

There was a connection somewhere, though. If only Longarm could call it to mind and make some sense out of it.

He shook his head, annoyed with himself for not being able to nail the thought down, and walked out of the barbershop.

Cowboys. Lots of cowboys. So what? In a town like Cimarron City, cowboys and soldiers and a few locals were exactly what you'd expect to find. And at this hour of the day all the soldiers from Good Enough would be attending to their duties. That would hold true regardless of race. White soldiers wouldn't be in town at this hour any more than the colored ones were. This time of day just naturally belonged to the townsmen and the cowboys who were passing by.

So what was it that was gnawing at Longarm's gut about the customers he was seeing in the café and now in the barber shop? He just couldn't quite pull the thought the last little way to the surface where he could look it over. Dammit.

He stepped inside the next general mercantile he came to, still puzzling over the half-formed thought that was worrying at him, and inspected the tobacco counter. The storekeeper had a nearly full box of the cheroots Longarm favored, so he examined one. The wrapper leaf was soft, indicting that the box was freshly opened and the cheroots not yet dried out so that the sweetness would leave the smoke.

"Three for a quarter, friend," the proprietor said.

Storekeeper, Longarm had just thought of this man as being? Licensed and legalized thief was more like it. In Denver he could buy these same smokes . . . he wasn't in Denver now, was he. And he was running kinda low. "I'll take a dollar's worth."

"Baker's dozen for a dollar," the man said, taking at least a little of the sting out. Longarm laid a cartwheel on the counter and made his selection of thirteen of the excellent little cheroots. The storekeeper offered a block of lumpy yellow lucifers gratis, but Longarm preferred his own fully formed and handy boxed matches to the old fashioned block kind.

"I'll take them things if you don't want 'em, neighbor," a voice said from over Longarm's shoulder.

It was the man who'd been standing beside Longarm in the breakfast line. "Sure thing." Longarm accepted the block of matches from the shopkeeper and passed them along to the cowboy.

"Thanks."

"No problem." If the man was bumming those nearly useless lucifers he must have run out of money after his night on the town. "Care for something to use them on?" Longarm offered.

The cowhand grinned, exposing the gaps in his teeth. "You bet, neighbor. Thanks."

Longarm provided cheroots for both of them, and the fellow from West Texas broke a lucifer off the corner of his block and actually managed to strike a flame from the crumbly sulfur tip. He held the flame to Longarm first, then bent his head to light his own smoke. "Aw, that's nice. Thanks."

"My pleasure."

The cowboy belched. He made a face. "Funny how somethin' that tastes so good the once don't taste worth a damn the second time."

Longarm laughed. He knew the feeling.

"Reckon I'd best start back now. Time my half the crew was gettin' home anyhow. There's another half snappin' and clawin' and wantin' to drink up whatever we left behind."

"I remember how that is," Longarm said.

"Been there, have you?"

"A time or two."

"Ayuh, I didn't think you looked much like one o' these plant-ass stay-at-homes," the cowboy drawled, not bothering to lower his voice so the storekeeper would not overhear. The cowboy obviously didn't give a crap if anyone heard or not.

"No, I move around plenty. Haven't worked cows in a long time though. I doubt I'd remember how."

"Cows ain't changed since you worked 'em, neighbor. Cows nor the men to work them, I don't reckon either one will ever change much."

Longarm smiled. "I'm sure you're right."

"Reckon I'll move along now. Thanks for the smoke."

"Any time."

The cowboy ankled off toward the door, a short, slightly built man with knees set so far apart a good-sized hog could walk underneath him and never touch on either side. Longarm smiled at the pleasant fellow and started to turn away. Then the smile froze in place, quite forgotten, and he snapped his fingers as the remainder of his errant thought swam up to the surface where he could see it.

"Hey," he called to the cowboy who was just then heading out the door. "Wait up there a second. There's something more I wanted to ask you." Longarm hurried out after the man.

Never did find him, though.

# Chapter 34

The bay horse loped smooth and easy along the mostly dry bed that was the Big Skull. Or whatever this sometime thread of water would be called. Longarm conceded that it wasn't necessary that the name of this particular gouge in the ground and the seasonal creek that ran through it be the same. The one thing he and everybody else around here was positive of was that it *wasn't* the Cimarron, no matter the name of the town.

Longarm had already made a scout along the creek bed out past Camp Good Enough. It was just like Capt. Hal Denis and the Texas cowboy both had told him he could expect. The grass was good out that way, but it was all occupied by dark-colored horses bearing the familiar U.S. brand on their near shoulders, along with assorted other scrapes, gouges, and brand marks, some of which meant something and some of which were accidental. The point was that everything for a good many miles in that direction was being used by the army for the Remount Service portion of Good Enough's official function here.

Cow outfits driving north onto the Ogallala government road and points beyond had to find their graze and water upstream from Cimarron City. Naturally the grass close in to town was cropped short from repeated use by the townspeople themselves. But further up Big Skull Wash there was no trouble finding grass and good water for beeves on the trail, the friendly Texan had explained.

And so Longarm was finding now.

He hadn't been able to see the herds before because of the twists and turns along the broad course of the Big Skull,

145

but once he started riding in that direction he started passing herds of cattle.

The first was located within three quarters of a mile from the western edge of Cimarron City, and several more herds were dotted here and there as he rode on along the wash.

What it came down to, he recognized very shortly, was that the beeves were put onto grass wherever there was a pothole of standing water with a few sprigs of grass growing around it. The trail crews loose-herded the stock while half of each crew at a time was released to ride down to town and whoop it up. Then that half would come back and stand watch over the bovines while the next batch went off to have their fun. It was a logical and easy way to handle things.

Except of course for this one niggling detail that shouldn't have been so.

And that was what Longarm needed to check on now.

He rode west at a steady lope for a solid half day, not pushing the bay horse but not letting up on it either. The animal was nicely conditioned. It worked up a good sweat but no serious lather, and neither its breathing nor its gait was labored.

Considering when he'd started and the pace he'd maintained, Longarm figured he had put a good thirty miles between himself and Cimarron City before he finally drew rein beside a pond of cool, shaded water.

The creek, when it was running as a creek, curved here, and on the miniature peninsula that was formed between a pair of oxbows there was a small stand of cottonwoods. Some condition of soil or current had scooped a deep depression into the creek bed, creating a pond to feed the roots of the cottonwoods with lifegiving moisture. And the cottonwoods in turn shaded and sheltered the pond, holding water loss to a minimum. It was like the trees and the pond were acting together for mutual defense against the elements.

Longarm figured this was as good a place to stop as any and a helluva lot better than most.

He unsaddled the bay and hobbled the animal, turning it loose to crop the lush, succulent grasses that grew on the creek bank just downstream from the cottonwood grove. His eyes were stinging and feeling gritty after going the night without sleep, so he spread his saddle blanket in the shade to serve as a pallet and used the seat of his McClellan for a pillow. He balanced his Stetson over his face to block out most of the light and let himself sink down into a welcome rest. He expected he would need to be feeling rested and ready come evening.

It was dusk when Longarm rode back into Cimarron City. The work day was done, and the section of the town that was set aside for use by the colored soldiers from Good Enough rang and clamored with the sounds of the nightly revelry.

There was money to be made over there. Lots of it. Which was one of the things that had puzzled Longarm ever since he got here. There aren't too many folks who are so high-principled—or so hate-filled, either one—that they are willing to kill that goose with the golden eggs.

That is one of the things that a man in Longarm's line of work learns early on: No SOB gores his own ox.

So if things are happening that don't fit the facts, it means that either those things aren't really happening . . . or you don't have all the facts.

Longarm was remembering that now.

He stepped down out of the saddle and started into the nearest saloon.

Harry Shelton was on his way out of the same doorway. The two met nose to nose and damn near collided.

"Long!"

"H'lo, Harry."

"I . . . I . . ." Harry gulped for air, his Adam's apple bobbing and quivering. "They said . . . somebody said . . . you was shot at last night, Long."

"That's right."

"They said . . . they said you went to the house looking for me."

"That's right too, Harry."

"I didn't . . . I mean, I never . . ."

"Last night I thought you were the one that shot at me, Harry."

"But I swear to you . . ."

"I believe you, Harry."

"You do?"

"It isn't that I think you wouldn't like to, Harry. We both know you'd like to kill me and brag on it after. But, Harry." Longarm smiled. "You don't have the guts to try me, Harry. Not even from behind."

"Jesus, Long. You . . ."

"Don't worry about it, Harry. Go home. Get Eddie to buy you a bottle to crawl into. If you drink enough, Harry, maybe you'll be able to convince yourself that you could've taken me. After I'm safely away from here, that is." Longarm's smile never wavered. But then it hadn't ever held any warmth in it to begin with.

"Jesus."

"Go home, Harry."

The man had turned pale sometime during the past few moments. He seemed shaky now. He trembled. Longarm could see in Harry's eyes a mixture of hate and terror. Harry desperately wished he had the courage to take Longarm on. But he simply didn't. His eyes filling with sudden tears of frustration, Harry Shelton stumbled blindly away, reeling off in the direction of Edna's whorehouse and oblivion.

"Kinda rough on that old boy tonight weren't you, mister?" a man asked.

"Kinda," Longarm agreed pleasantly. "You want some of it next?"

"No, mister, I was just asking."

"No harm in asking," Longarm said. "Usually."

The customer who'd put his nose where it didn't belong turned away from a nearly full mug of beer and walked out, apparently determining that another saloon might be a healthier environment than this one.

"Nice to see you tonight, Marshal," the bartender said. "I sure hope you'll let me keep on feeling that way."

"What? Oh. Sorry. I, uh, sometimes get a mite testy where Harry Shelton is concerned."

"Y'know, Marshal, I'd kinda suspected that already."

"I'll try not to run anybody else off."

"I'd appreciate that."

"Seen Charley Hamer tonight?"

"Not yet, but he's due. You and him aren't going to have another fight, are you?"

Longarm grinned. "The way I remember it, friend, me and Charley never actually got around to having us a first fight. Be hard to have a second when there ain't been a first. But if Charley wants, I'll sure go hunt up a horse for him to tangle with."

"Ha. That's a good one, Marshal. Here y'go. Have a beer while you wait. Charley won't be more'n ten, fifteen minutes, I'd wager."

"Thanks." Longarm paid for the beer and helped himself to a pickled egg and a handful of peanuts from the free lunch spread. He was hungry, not having taken the time to buy a lunch to carry with him when he rode out earlier, but he wanted to wait and see Hamer before he did anything else.

Business before pleasure.

And he had quite a lot of business to tend to before this night was ended.

# Chapter 35

She came outside at 9:30 or so. Longarm was not sure of the time because it was too dark to read the Ingersol without striking a match. And anyway he really didn't care. He was willing to wait as long as proved necessary. Or to start tap-tapping on window glass with softly thrown pebbles if that was what it took.

Fortunately he wasn't required to go to that extent. He noticed an upstairs lamp blown out in a room above the kitchen and a minute or so later the back door swung open. A pale, ethereal form came floating through the night air like mist drifting over a dark, still pond.

"Don't be frightened, Victoria. It's me."

She stopped, smiled. "Longarm?"

"I took a chance you might come out t' sit again tonight."

She hurried forward into the shadowy interior of the carriage shed and found him sprawled on the upholstered driver's seat of the utility wagon. Longarm helped her onto the box beside him, and Victoria came into his arms with a breathless intensity. Her kisses were fervid, and she began tugging at his buttons almost immediately.

He chuckled and held her away a bit. "Slow down, lady. We got all night again if that's what it takes t' satisfy the both of us."

"Oh, I'm so glad to see you here, Longarm. Last night, when you left, I thought sure you wouldn't come again. I thought . . . never mind what I thought. I was wrong. You did come back."

"Said I would if I could, didn't I?"

"I've heard lines from men before, dear."

"Not from me you haven't." He supposed he ought to feel guilty that he was using her like this. Somehow he couldn't much work up much in that line of feeling though, particularly when she stripped off her nightdress and commenced to grope at his crotch while rubbing her titties back and forth on him.

"You aren't gonna leak on my coat, are you?"

"No, silly. I just finished the evening feeding. I'm dry as dry can be. See for yourself." With that she shifted position and pressed a nipple against his lips. Turned out she was pretty nigh right. All he got out of her was a slow dribble of the sweet, thin fluid. "Satisfied now?" she demanded.

"Not hardly."

"I mean about my milk, dummy."

"Oh." He feigned a dawning of comprehension and then grinned, snaking an arm around her tiny waist and drawing her into his lap. "About that one thing, I'm satisfied. But as for this . . ." He slid a hand between her thighs, his fingers probing and finding a warm and already moist opening inside the soft, curly nest of hair that covered her mound.

"Ooo!"

"Hurt?"

"Anything but." She wriggled, settling herself deeper onto his touch. She groaned. Her eyes drooped closed and her jaw went slack as Victoria drew inside herself in response to the sensations he was causing in her. After a few moments more she began to shudder and her breath came quick and hard. He could feel the lips of her pussy clench and throb around his intruding hand as Victoria built swiftly toward a climax. When she came she cried out aloud and went rigid as a drawn longbow. Then just as suddenly she went completely limp, melting against him and collapsing there. She didn't move.

"Victoria? You all right?" It took her a minute to come around again. The intensity of her climax had been so strong that she momentarily passed out. It was a reaction Longarm had seen before. But not often. It was, he admitted, kinda flattering whenever it happened. Made a fella feel good to be able to do that much for a woman. This time was no exception to that. "Are you all right?" he repeated when he was sure she could hear.

She nodded. And shuddered lightly in a small after shock of pleasure. Then she smiled and stroked his face and his neck. "Wow."

"Yeah," he said, "I reckon you're all right."

"My turn," she said.

"I kinda thought you just had a turn."

"You know what I mean, dear." She helped him off with his clothes, and they stepped over the seat back to the wagon bed where Longarm already had a thick buffalo robe laid out and the blanket from the surrey laid on top of that, buffalo robes tending to tickle if you sit on one bare-assed and the coarse hair works up into the crack of one's butt.

Victoria knelt on the soft pallet he had created. Longarm was still standing. With a smile she pulled him nearer so that his crotch was on a level with her head. "Mmm. Nice. No, don't move. Not yet, please."

She took him into her mouth, mumbling and muttering and gently tasting of him.

"Not that way," he said, his responses to what she was doing already commencing to rise toward a point of no return.

"But I want you here, dear. I want to taste it. I want to feel the way you bump and throb when it spurts out."

"Next time then. Right now . . ." He bent, forcing her off of him and down on her back.

Victoria didn't object. She was pliant, as malleable as gold. And as valuable.

She opened herself to him, and Longarm plunged deep inside her slim body. He felt her wrap herself tightly around him, arms and legs and mouth all clinging to him as resolute as a leech.

She gasped as Longarm's cock filled her. She was able to accommodate him, though. He didn't have to hold back with her.

Victoria writhed and moaned as Longarm began stroking back and forth. He went slowly at first, wanting to prolong his own pleasure as long as possible. But the combination of Victoria's intense body heat and the lubricous friction of her flesh wrapped so tightly around him soon defeated his plans to make the experience last.

He felt the swelling rise of sensation start deep within his balls and expand until the pressure was beyond denial. He exploded with a wildly gushing release, tensing and shuddering out of control, slamming his belly hard against hers as if trying to drive her through the wagon floor, grabbing at her with his hands and cruelly kneading her soft flesh in his clenching fists, bucking and thrusting and riding the tiger.

Through it all Victoria grunted and squealed and humped hard against him, taking everything Longarm had to give and returning it every bit as vigorously.

He shuddered and stiffened, ramming himself as deep within her as he could force himself. Then he collapsed on top of her. Victoria sighed happily and put her arms around him. She took his weight onto her own diminutive body and stroked and patted him, clucking and muttering to him wordlessly and covering whatever of his flesh that she could reach with kisses light as a butterfly's wings in flight.

"Are you . . . ?"

"Shh, shh, darling, I'm fine. You didn't hurt me. You couldn't hurt me. Not that way. Not ever that way. Didn't you know, dear, that that is what woman's body is meant to do? You'll never cause me pain that way." She stroked and kissed him over and over again.

Longarm felt himself grow drowsy and he did not care. He let his eyes sag closed, let himself remain limp and sated atop Victoria's lithe and lovely body. He felt the warmth of her, and that warmth surrounded him in more ways than just the one.

Still socketed deep within the center of her being, Longarm drifted off to sleep.

# Chapter 36

Victoria sat up in a cross-legged position, smiled, and wiped her mouth with the back of her hand. "Yum," she said.

Longarm made a face.

Victoria laughed. "Men aren't expected to find it tasty, silly. But I happen to like it, thank you."

"I ain't complaining," he pointed out. "Comes t' that, ma'am, I reckon I'd be willing to provide 'bout all of it you'd care t' drink."

"What a lovely offer, dear. Thank you." With a grin she leaned down and lightly kissed the limp, wet thing that nested in a patch of dark fur at Longarm's middle. After he woke a little earlier she had insisted that he honor his promise and hold still while she played with him there. Not that it'd been all that hard for her to convince him. The girl was almighty good, any old way he turned her.

"Hand me my coat there, would you?" She complied and he brought out a cheroot and match. Victoria wadded some bits of clothing into a ball for them to share as a pillow, then tucked herself down at his side while Longarm smoked in the cool night air.

"Tell me 'bout yourself," he suggested.

"Oh, there isn't all that much to tell. Certainly nothing interesting."

"If it's about you I'll be interested."

"You sound like you mean that."

"Only because I do."

She smiled and teasingly licked his right nipple.

"We'll get t' that again," he promised. "Just give me a few minutes t' recover. Meantime, tell me about yourself.

All I know is that you got a husband and a baby. An' that I'm damned lucky you're out here with me 'stead o' being in there with them."

For a moment Victoria looked serious. "It sounds awful when you put it that way, doesn't it?"

"I didn't mean for it to." That was a lie. He told himself that it was for good purpose. The truth, though, was that he wanted her to feel guilty enough that she would be impelled to provide explanations. "I just want t' know everything about you, that's all."

Victoria lay silent at his side for several minutes, long enough that he thought it wasn't going to work, that she was not going to open up and talk freely to him after all. After a while, though, she began to whisper in the silence of the night. She lay staring toward the shed roof while she did so, probably finding it easier to speak if she was not looking at him while she did.

Hers was a marriage of convenience rather than love. In fact, she had never slept with Col. Willard Sherman. That was the colonel's choice, not hers. She had come into the marriage willing to act in all the ways that a wife must, fully prepared to keep her share of a bargain. But Sherman had never once made any advance toward her. Her bedroom door had never been locked, but the knob was never tried. That was a revelation that made Longarm bite his lip to keep from blurting out a comment. What sort of man could . . . would . . . damn!

The child's father had been one of her father's employees. A dashing, handsome, devil-may-care sort, all charm and good looks. But when Victoria MacKay found herself with child, the soon-to-be papa found himself with a burning desire to see what lay past yonder hill. She learned he was gone when she went to his tent to find him. And found that he had "willed" her to one of his chums in the work crew. The man had actually granted his "rights" to Victoria's body to this other fellow as payment for a small debt.

Victoria had been humiliated twice over. It was bad enough that she was unwed and with child. It was all the worse now that everyone on her father's crew knew about her disgrace.

The men all had to be let go, of course. Her father had insisted. But the disgrace was his as much as hers once that happened. She was convinced that her situation forced him to retire much earlier than he would have wanted. She blamed herself for driving her beloved da to drink.

Longarm asked gently leading questions now and then. Angus MacKay had been an engineer before his retirement. He specialized in surveys. But no more. All of that was long done with.

And Sherman? She didn't know how her husband had known of the MacKays and their family shame. The colonel had addressed himself to Angus first. Probably in a barroom somewhere. That was where her da spent all his time then. Da it was who brought the man home. And his proposition.

Victoria had been shamed yet again by Sherman's proposal. He would agree to marry Victoria and to give his name to the child she carried. She and her da would agree to live with him and present to the world a picture of domestic bliss. Victoria would be expected to serve as hostess and, at least in public, companion. Her father . . . she frowned when she related this part. She was under the impression that something was asked of her father too. But she did not know what it might have been. She only knew that for a brief period after the wedding ceremony her da had remained sober. Not willingly but sober. And then he and the colonel went off together for a few days. She didn't know where they might possibly have gone, after all. They all were living here at The Folly by then, and the men were not absent long enough for a trip to Pueblo or Trinidad or any other place that she could think of. And that was before Camp Good Enough and Cimarron City were here. Then it had only been raw empty plains that could be seen from the bluff. Emptiness below the house and emptiness within the house, but there The Folly sat in all its seeming splendor.

Anyway, she said, her husband and her father took that one brief trip together. And after that her father had rarely drawn a sober breath. Hardly a one.

She was crying by now. Longarm cuddled and petted and kissed her. And encouraged her to talk more.

156

She knew very little about the man who was her husband. She thought he had friends in the military. She had seen his outgoing correspondence—he was a compulsive writer of letters, she claimed—and most of them were addressed to colonels and generals and the like, some at army posts here or there, some apparently retired from active service, as Colonel Sherman himself was, because the men he wrote to most often were now officers in railroad corporations. Did she recall any of the names and corporations? She shrugged. Of course. She named several, none of which were familiar to Longarm.

Her father now spent his time in a mild stupor. Her husband spent his time in correspondence. Or—she didn't mean to be catty, honestly she didn't, but the truth was the truth—or closeted behind locked doors with Carlotta and Serena. The three of them in there together. Doing things. At night she could hear them. She despised having to listen to them. That was one of the things that drove her out here to the carriage shed nearly every evening after the baby was fed.

Longarm understood that she was jealous, never mind that the marriage was one of convenience. Victoria was a young woman who had been introduced to the pleasures of her body and then those pleasures were suddenly denied her. No wonder she had been so eager to come into his arms when Longarm presented himself before her.

She hated, too, the fact that the colonel and his two mistresses could exclude her simply by speaking the Spanish that she did not comprehend. Victoria felt lonely and more than a little frightened. And she was becoming more and more uncomfortable of late without understanding why. It was just that something, she didn't know what, but something was bothering the colonel. There never had been affection or good will in the house. But here lately there was tension and snappishness, and Victoria was afraid that if the colonel's plans did not come to fruition, whatever those plans might be, her husband might do something extreme. No, she had no idea what. Nor did she have any basis for her fears. She only knew that she could sense hidden capacities for violence, and she was frightened.

Longarm kissed and cuddled her some more, and after a bit her trembling subsided.

The girl had given him more than he ever expected when he came here. He had fully intended to use her in any way that he could. He felt less guilt about that than he probably should have. What she told him, though . . . it all fit nicely with what he had already begun to suspect. At least in broad outline, it did. There were a great many details yet to be fill in before the picture would be clear. But the shape of it was nearly recognizable now. And he thought he knew where to find the remainder of what he needed. In the meantime . . .

To assuage his own conscience if nothing else, Longarm paid for the information by giving back pleasure. After Victoria had time to recover from the uneasiness of her storytelling he bent over her and began the slow and pleasant tasks of arousing her body once more to a fevered pitch of excitement, this time bringing her to one shaking, shuddering climax after another until she begged him to let her come down off that razor's edge that separates pleasure from pain. He relented and gave her a few minutes to rest. And then started in on her again.

# Chapter 37

Longarm missed breakfast. In fact, by the time he finally woke up he was damned lucky to make it to the officers' mess in time for lunch. What he really needed, he thought, was a bath and a shave, but there would be time enough for that sort of thing later. In the meantime there was work to be done.

This all would have been much, much easier, he knew, if there was a telegraph line to Good Enough. Still, he thought he had enough of a handle on it that he could confirm what he had to right here in the area. With a little bit of luck, that is.

There was no sign of Hal Denis in the mess tent when Longarm got there, and he had no desire whatsoever to eat in the company of the human flotsam that the post had collected to serve as its junior officers. Longarm settled for grabbing a chunk of boiled beef and a handful of dinner rolls—who could ask for a better breakfast than that—and hiking off to the headquarters tent.

Sergeant Prior gave Longarm a sheepish look when the tall deputy made his appearance there.

"Something wrong, Sergeant?"

"We . . . that is to say, sir, I . . . owe you an apology."

"You do?"

"About the other night, sir. When you were shot at?"

Longarm had no idea what in hell the man was getting at.

"We was keeping an eye on your backside, sir. As best we could in that town, that is. And then that woman went an' shot at you. My boys sure as hell hadn't expected that,

159

sir. But we like to let you get killed. And to make matters worse, sir, we let her get away without anybody seeing who it was that did it, sir. All they seen was that it was a woman."

Longarm grunted. Once or twice he'd had a faint sense that he was being watched. But never anything serious. The sergeant's men were very good indeed. As for the ambusher . . . "Never mind, Sergeant. I know who it was."

"Yes, sir. You wanting to see the captain now, sir?"

"If that would be convenient, yes."

"Please wait here, sir." Prior was gone only briefly. When he returned he beckoned for Longarm to follow.

Hal Denis greeted him with obvious pleasure. "It's about time you showed up here, Longarm. I've been wondering how your investigation is coming along."

Longarm took the seat Denis pointed to. He crossed his legs and offered the captain a cheroot before he got down to business. "Pretty well, I'd say. Except maybe for a question o' jurisdiction. I know who's behind the problems, and I'm pretty sure I know why. It's just that I'm not sure there's been a federal law broken."

Captain Denis frowned over his cheroot for a moment in deep thought. "Perhaps you should tell me about it, Longarm. Talking it out might make you feel better."

Longarm chuckled. "That'd be one solution, wouldn't it."

"What?"

"You don't have to pretend you don't understand, Hal. I don't mind what you're thinking. I say it in this office, other ears pick up the message. And next thing you know there's a visit takes place in the night. I can't say that it'd be the worst thing ever happened. And if it turns out there's no other way, Hal, maybe I will sit in this chair right here and tell you everything I suspect. But I'd sure like to think that you and me got better ways to handle things than that."

Denis shrugged, but did not bother to apologize.

Beyond the tent wall Longarm thought he heard a muted shuffle that might have been a shoe sole moving on hard-packed earth. Or might have been nothing at all.

"You told me once that you'd do whatever you could t' help, Hal. Did you mean it?"

160

"Of course I meant it," Denis said.

"Then let me run some names past you."

"Shoot."

There were only a few. They reached pay dirt with the name of Brigadier General Bernard Moncrief.

"I know Bernard, Longarm. He's retired now, of course. I served under him when I was a shavetail. He was my immediate commander. A good man. Our wives were close friends. I've kept in touch with Bernard off and on over the years. In fact I heard from him recently. He's on the board of directors of some railroad company. I forget which one. For some reason he expects to be traveling to Cimarron City in another month or two." Denis smiled. "He said I should save him a seat at the card table one evening when he is in the vicinity. Can you see me trying to teach whist to a pack of imbeciles like my officers here? But I suppose I shall have to. It's either that or let Bernard claim he's bested me. Can't have that, can I?"

"No, I reckon you couldn't. You say he's some high-up officer with this railroad?"

"You know the sort of thing. Generals command respect. They give any venture an aura of respectability. And that helps draw in the investors. Most of these railroad schemes sink without ever laying a rail in place, of course. Which doesn't seem to stop new ones from cropping up underfoot constantly. Doesn't seem to much discourage the investors either. For Bernard's sake I just hope he is taking his compensation in cash rather than stock."

Longarm grunted. People like Hal Denis and this Moncrief might care about such things. Longarm was only interested in them as they applied to his own work. "He's coming to Cimarron City, though, not to Good Enough."

"Same difference, wouldn't you say?"

Longarm wouldn't, in fact. But he didn't say so. He merely grunted again and went through the rest of his short list of names with the friendly officer. Finally he stood. "You've been a big help, Hal. Thanks."

Denis looked puzzled. "I can't see that I've done anything to help."

"That's all right. You have. Take my word for it."

161

"About what we discussed earlier . . ."

"If it comes t' that, Hal, we'll talk it over then. But I hope it don't."

"Of course. Good luck, Longarm. Can we look forward to your company at dinner tonight? Some of the officers are taking their shotguns and going out for prairie chickens. That is one of the few things they are capable of. It's quite a treat in the mess when they are successful."

"I'll make it if I can, thanks, but don't count on me." Count on him? Huh. Prairie hen is edible, all right. But you have to be mighty fond of the flavor of sage. It wasn't Longarm's idea of a special treat. He put his Stetson on and headed for the doorway, then stopped and turned back.

"Yes, Longarm?"

"I keep forgetting t' ask you, Hal. Where'd the name Camp Good Enough come from?"

"You know, I've often wondered that myself. Wish I could tell you." Denis smiled and went back to his paperwork.

Longarm followed the canvas corridor to the front where Sergeant Prior already had the bay horse waiting for him.

"Sir."

"Yes, Sergeant?"

"The captain, he didn't want to say anything. He's about half shamed. But this post, sir, was named by Colonel Ledbetter up to Fort Lyons. It's called Good Enough because bad as it is it's good enough for a bunch of niggers."

"I see. Well, at least it's a name that makes some sort of sense. And you don't have to carry a post name honoring some dead hero who would have despised you if he'd ever had to take you into his command."

"There is that, sir, isn't there," Prior agreed.

"Good day, sergeant."

"And to you, sir."

Longarm swung onto the bay and bumped it into a lope in the direction of Cimarron City, which wasn't named nearly so logically as Camp Good Enough.

# Chapter 38

"Longarm. Darling." Victoria seemed overjoyed to see him, even in the middle of the afternoon. She came up onto her tiptoes to give him a welcoming kiss and invited him inside without hesitation.

"Long? What are you doing here?" Willard Sherman was in the parlor, standing now with a newspaper in his hands. He was wearing carpet slippers and a faded smoking jacket.

"Sorry, Colonel, I didn't mean t' disturb you. I came t' see Mr. MacKay."

"I am afraid the old gentleman is under the weather today, Marshal. Perhaps you could call again?"

Longarm smiled. "I really do need to see him today. Victoria, ask your da t' come downstairs if you please."

She nodded and gathered her skirts to leave the room.

"Victoria!" The colonel's voice was sharp. "You will do no such thing until or unless I give my permission."

"But . . ."

"I insist on it."

The woman looked helplessly from her husband to her lover and back again. She obviously wanted to obey Longarm. But just as obviously felt obligated to do as Sherman bid her.

The two Mexican girls had materialized from somewhere in the back. Longarm looked at them. "Carlotta, fetch old Mr. Angus down, please."

The girl gave him a stricken look. "I cannot, señor. My master say. I cannot."

"Very well, Carlotta, I . . ." Longarm bit the words off

163

short. And began to grin. "Thank you, Carlotta. You just solved a big problem for me."

"Que?"

"Never mind." Longarm gave Sherman a smug look and walked over to the foot of the stairs. "Angus, Angus MacKay," he bellowed just as loud as he could. "This is Deputy United States Marshal Custis Long. I've come to talk to you."

"I protest this disgraceful intrusion into my home, Marshal," Sherman snapped. "You have no right to be here without a warrant. I insist that you withdraw immediately or I shall be forced to carry my case to your superiors."

Longarm laughed. "You ever think about reading law, Willard? Maybe you ought to. It's amazing all the stuff you'd learn."

"Get out. Get out of my house. I demand it."

"I was invited in by your wife, Colonel. I'm not trespassing."

"You are now. I insist that you leave."

Longarm tilted his head back and roared, "Angus MacKay, get down here right now."

"You can't do this, Long."

"I'm already doing it, Willard."

"I shall evict you by force if I must."

"Any time you reckon you're man enough to get the job done, Willard, you go ahead an' have at it." He looked up again. "MacKay, don't make me come up there and drag you down. I'll arrest you if I have to."

"On what charge?" Sherman shrilled.

"Material witness t' start with. Who knows what could come after."

Victoria stiffened when she heard that. Now she was being torn in three different directions, loyalty to the husband who was hers in name only, affection for a newfound lover, and most of all a deep and abiding love for the father she already felt guilty about ruining. "Longarm. No!"

"I got to talk with him, Victoria. Your da has the last keys that'll unlock a problem. I got to get them from him."

"Get out. Get *out*!" Sherman was screaming now. The two Mexican girls were crying and clinging to one another.

164

Victoria didn't look like she was doing so very damn well either. Longarm figured the household was right well aware that he'd come t' call, all right.

"MacKay. Get down here."

"I am coming, sir. I surrender myself into your custody." MacKay's voice was weak but determined. The old man stood at the head of the stairs with all the dignity he could muster. He had pulled on a suit coat and made a poor attempt to knot a tie at his throat even though there was no collar attached to his rumpled, sweat-stained shirt. His shoes had no laces in them and his trousers had no belt. But the old fellow stood as tall and proud as he was able when he started haltingly down the stairs.

"No," Sherman shrieked. "No. You'll ruin everything. Go back, you fool, go back."

MacKay was paying no attention to his son-in-law. He inched down one slow step at a time lest he totter and fall.

"You can't." Willard Sherman reached inside his coat and pulled out a pocket revolver. It was a tiny thing, nickel-plated and silly-looking. But deadly enough for all of that. The suddenly desperate colonel pointed the little gun at Angus MacKay who was exposed on the open staircase.

Longarm grabbed his own Colt out, but quick as he was Victoria was even quicker. While Longarm's attention had been on MacKay, hers must have been on Sherman right along. By the time Longarm reached the grips of his revolver Victoria had the globe of a lamp in her hand and was swinging it. The glass reservoir crashed against Sherman's gun and shattered, sending shards of broken glass and a spray of whale oil . . . and more to the point the gun itself . . . flying. Victoria left her husband standing there in disbelief and raced for the stairs to help her father.

Willard Sherman looked wildly about, but his revolver had skittered out of sight beneath the furniture. He snatched up a fancy cane that had been leaning against his reading chair. A swift twist of the handle, and the barrel of the cane was stripped away to reveal a sword blade.

"Damn you," he shouted at Longarm. "Damn you."

"Drop that silly thing, man, and hush yourself while I

165

get t' the bottom o' this," Longarm warned casually. After all, nobody in his right mind was gonna take cold steel and charge into the face of a drawn and ready Colt revolver.

Longarm turned to see if Victoria and MacKay were all right. The Mexican girls had long since fled screaming toward the kitchen. Likely they were huddled in the pantry or some such place. They could be collected and talked to later. Right now, though, he needed to sit down with Angus MacKay and get the rest of the answers he needed.

"Longarm. Look out!" Victoria's scream cut through his plans.

Willard Sherman had gone berserk. Or else the man had been so conditioned by his years of army service that he never stopped and realized how just plain stupid it was to think that steel could face powder.

The man was actually charging Longarm with the sword waving wildly overhead. Just like on some cavalry practice field. Not at *all* like it was done in real combat. This poor dumb SOB must never have faced genuine danger in his life.

On the other hand, Longarm hadn't time enough to give him any lessons in reality.

And Sherman showed every apparent intent of running Long through.

Reluctantly—but only a very little—Longarm took careful aim and shot Col. Willard Sherman just about an inch beneath the point of his widow's peak. The man was dead before his body ever quit running, and the sword clattered harmlessly onto the floorboards.

"Reckon I don't have t' worry about that shaky jurisdiction question now, do I?" Longarm muttered to himself as he replaced the spent cartridge with a fresh one and pushed the Thunderer back into his holster.

"Are you all right, Victoria?"

She nodded. And began helping her da down the stairs.

# Chapter 39

"I hate t' say it," Longarm admitted, "but in a way I'm glad it worked out like this." He took a sip of the coffee Victoria had made. Carlotta and Serena were still hiding in the pantry—he'd checked on them just to make sure—but he figured they would keep right there until he wanted them.

His biggest problem to this point had been in trying to convince old Angus MacKay that he wasn't going to arrest him. Not immediately, anyway. They would have to see about what happened later.

Not that that had been any drawback to getting the old man to talk. MacKay had been so guilt-ridden and nervous that he would have confessed everything even if his own words took him to a gallows. But then some folks just aren't much cut out for lies and criminal activity.

Longarm nodded to Victoria's offer of a refill. "If the man'd had sense enough to keep himself still instead o' chasing after me with that oversized carving knife, I doubt he would ever have served more'n six months in prison. If that. I mean, he didn't do all that much himself. He got others to do the things he wanted done. Like you, Mr. MacKay."

"I thought you said Willard strangled that woman in town."

"Hell, I'm sure he did. Pretty much had t' be him. But nobody ever woulda proved it on him. For sure I couldn't. And nobody else cared. As for the rest o' the stuff that brought me here, all he done was spread lies and rumors around trying t' cause trouble so the army'd pull out and relocate that post before it became a permanent thing and reservation boundaries had t' be laid out."

"That's where my benchmark would have come in?"

"Uh huh. Though t' tell you the truth, I hadn't been even close to figuring out what all he was up to. I didn't have the whole of it until you explained about that. Then it all fit together pretty as you please." The matter involving a surveyor's benchmark had been Angus MacKay's contribution to Sherman's scheme. But there again the colonel had had MacKay do the actual work of relocating the mark. That was very likely a federal crime; a crime that was committed by Angus MacKay and not Willard Sherman.

All Longarm thought he could even charge Sherman with was involuntary servitude. He could, in effect, claim that Sherman was holding Carlotta and Serena in illegal slavery. After all, the girls referred to Sherman as their master. And it wasn't exactly unknown for a desperately poor Mexican peon to sell a daughter now and then. Even if the charge could be made to stick, though, the man would have drawn little punishment if any.

It was his own stupidity that cost him his life.

As for Sherman's plans, Longarm wasn't able to judge. But he suspected Sherman had panicked before it was really necessary then too.

The colonel's original idea was for MacKay to move the government benchmark and thereby "move" the boundary between Colorado and the Indian Territories.

Through his network of former army cronies, Sherman had known that a railroad intended building in this direction. And he knew as well that the roadbed would have to be constructed on the hard caprock that formed the bluff where The Folly now sat. Because of questions of both grade and stability, a railroad constructed through here would not be able to cross Big Skull Wash without extraordinary expense, possibly expense enough to make an underfinanced company change its route plans. And Sherman was counting on there being a railroad here.

His scheme was to gain control of the caprock land that the railroad would have to cross and then sell the land to the company, taking stock if he had to in lieu of some of the cash. Willard Sherman had had a touchingly stubborn faith in the ability of his former companions in arms to turn a profit in business.

But first he had to secure control of the land in question. And, in fact, the caprock lay in the federally administered Indian Territories. A railroad wanting right of way across federal land would only have to ask, and title would be freely granted by the government in exchange for development of the new rail lines.

Sherman could only lay claim to the land if it was in the state of Colorado and subject to preemption.

And since he couldn't move the caprock into Colorado, he picked up the hem of Colorado's skirts and tugged it over far enough to cover the caprock, in essence moving the boundary line dividing Colorado from the I.T. when he had that benchmark relocated to where he wanted it.

Having done that, however, his fear was that a survey by government crews laying out a permanent military installation at Good Enough would expose the deception of the wandering benchmark and send the whole scheme up in a puff of smoke.

Longarm's opinion was that once again the poor sap had had touching but misplaced faith in the government's efficiency. It really was no more likely that an army surveyor would have discovered the problem than that a railroad surveyor would.

Still, believing that his plan was in danger, Sherman reacted by trying to make the vicinity so uncomfortable for the army that the post would be moved.

As for the town, Sherman really didn't much care if it stayed where it was or not so long as no one questioned its site. In fact, of course, every resident of Cimarron City was illegally squatting on federal land in the I.T. regardless of their mistaken belief, thanks to Willard Sherman, that they were in Colorado here. He certainly hadn't been inclined to correct them.

Longarm wondered if anybody was going to have to move them all off. Or if the government would prefer that a blind eye be turned to the whole thing since the town served both Camp Good Enough and the Ogallala Trail just as things stood. It wasn't a point Longarm intended to bring up.

As for the vigilance committee, that was all a matter of rumor started by Sherman. Charley Hamer had been entirely honest when he assured Longarm there was no such thing. Martha Freeman had been equally honest when she said she "knew" there was a committee. Willard Sherman, acting mostly through Carlotta and Serena, had been a busy boy when it came to rumor and innuendo. He had done it often enough to actually create incidents of racial violence.

Given enough time and enough support from his friends still in uniform, the man might very well have been able to succeed in his plan to have Good Enough relocated.

As for the future of the railroad that was headed by General Moncrief, Longarm neither knew nor cared. If the line did build through here, though, they would do so a damn sight cheaper than they might have, because now they wouldn't have to buy right of way from Colonel Sherman. All they would have to do would be to apply to the government for a land grant, and with Moncrief's connections that should prove to be no barrier whatsoever.

"What I think you oughta do, Angus," Longarm said, "is go out an' put that mark back where you got it."

"You're sure?"

"If you do it quick, like before the government sends in another survey team, I'd say there wouldn't be no evidence remaining then that any wrong was ever done."

"You aren't arresting me?"

"Will there be any evidence against you do I decide t' ride out and look at that benchmark?"

"That depends on how quickly you ride out, doesn't it?"

"Oh, I ain't in a big hurry t' get away from here." Longarm looked at Victoria and winked. Of course something would have to be done about her husband's body. And eventually he would have to get around to coaxing the Mexican girls out of the pantry and calming them. But, no, he wasn't in any real big hurry to leave.

"Would you mind if I were to borrow your horse, Marshal?"

"Reckon it couldn't hurt anything."

MacKay left, acting stronger and more sure of himself than at any time since Longarm first met him.

170

Victoria took Longarm's hand and squeezed it. She was crying again, but those were tears of relief from knowing her father was safe from the threat of prison. And Longarm thought he could come up with something to distract her from her other worries, at least for the time being. He smiled and tugged, and she came willing to sit in his lap and tuck her head beneath his chin.

Watch for

**LONGARM AND THE CHEYENNE KID**

164th in the bold LONGARM series
from Jove

*Coming in August!*

Fury knew something was wrong long before he saw the wagon train spread out, unmoving, across the plains in front of him.

From miles away, he had noticed the cloud of dust kicked up by the hooves of the mules and oxen pulling the wagons. Then he had seen that tan-colored pall stop and gradually be blown away by the ceaseless prairie wind.

It was the middle of the afternoon, much too early for a wagon train to be stopping for the day. Now, as Fury topped a small, grass-covered ridge and saw the motionless wagons about half a mile away, he wondered just what kind of damn fool was in charge of the train.

Stopping out in the open without even forming into a circle was like issuing an invitation to the Sioux, the Cheyenne, or the Pawnee. War parties roamed these plains all the time, just looking for a situation as tempting as this one.

Fury reined in, leaned forward in his saddle, and thought about it. Nothing said he had to go help those pilgrims. They might not even want his help.

But from the looks of things, they needed his help, whether they wanted it or not.

He heeled the rangy lineback dun into a trot toward the wagons. As he approached, he saw figures scurrying back and forth around the canvas-topped vehicles. Looked sort of like an anthill after you stomp it.

Fury pulled the dun to a stop about twenty feet from the lead wagon. Near it, a man was stretched out on the ground with so many men and women gathered around him that Fury could only catch a glimpse of him through the crowd. When some of the men turned to look at him, Fury said, "Howdy. Thought it looked like you were having trouble."

"Damn right, mister," one of the pilgrims snapped. "And if you're of a mind to give us more, I'd advise against it."

Fury crossed his hands on the saddlehorn and shifted in the saddle, easing his tired muscles. "I'm not looking to cause trouble for anybody," he said mildly.

He supposed he might appear a little threatening to a bunch of immigrants who had never been any farther west than the Mississippi. Several days had passed since his face had known the touch of the razor, and his rough-hewn features could be a little intimidating even without the beard stubble. Besides that, he was well armed with a Colt's Third Model Dragoon pistol holstered on his right hip, a Bowie knife sheathed on his left, and a Sharps carbine in the saddleboot under his right thigh. And he had the look of a man who knew how to use all three weapons.

A husky, broad-shouldered six-footer, John Fury's height was apparent even on horseback. He wore a broad-brimmed, flat-crowned black hat, a blue work shirt, and fringed buckskin pants that were tucked into high-topped black boots. As he swung down from the saddle, a man's voice, husky with strain, called out, "Who's that? Who are you?"

The crowd parted, and Fury got a better look at the figure on the ground. It was obvious that he was the one who had spoken. There was blood on the man's face, and from the twisted look of him as he lay on the ground, he was busted up badly inside.

Fury let the dun's reins trail on the ground, confident that the horse wouldn't go anywhere. He walked over to the injured man and crouched beside him. "Name's John Fury," he said.

The man's breath hissed between his teeth, whether in pain or surprise Fury couldn't have said. "Fury? I heard of you."

Fury just nodded. Quite a few people reacted that way when they heard his name.

"I'm . . . Leander Crofton. Wagonmaster of . . . this here train." The man struggled to speak. He appeared to be in his fifties and had a short, grizzled beard and the leathery skin of a man who had spent nearly his whole life outdoors. His pale blue eyes were narrowed in a permanent squint.

"What happened to you?" Fury asked.

"It was a terrible accident—" began one of the men standing nearby, but he fell silent when Fury cast a hard glance at him. Fury had asked Crofton, and that was who he looked toward for the answer.

Crofton smiled a little, even though it cost him an effort. "Pulled a damn fool stunt," he said. "Horse nearly stepped on a rattler, and I let it rear up and get away from me. Never figured the critter'd spook so easy." The wagonmaster paused to draw a breath. The air rattled in his throat and chest. "Tossed me off and stomped all over me. Not the first time I been stepped on by a horse, but then a couple of the oxen pullin' the lead wagon got me, too, 'fore the driver could get 'em stopped."

"God forgive me, I . . . I am so sorry." The words came in a tortured voice from a small man with dark curly hair and a beard. He was looking down at Crofton with lines of misery etched onto his face.

"Wasn't your fault, Leo," Crofton said. "Just . . . bad luck."

Fury had seen men before who had been trampled by horses. Crofton was in a bad way, and Fury could tell by the look in the man's eyes that Crofton was well aware of it. The wagonmaster's chances were pretty slim.

"Mind if I look you over?" Fury asked. Maybe he could do something to make Crofton's passing a little easier, anyway.

One of the other men spoke before Crofton had a chance to answer. "Are you a doctor, sir?" he asked.

Fury glanced up at him, saw a slender, middle-aged man with iron-gray hair. "No, but I've patched up quite a few hurt men in my time."

"Well, I am a doctor," the gray-haired man said. "And I'd appreciate it if you wouldn't try to move or examine Mr. Crofton. I've already done that, and I've given him

179

some laudanum to ease the pain."

Fury nodded. He had been about to suggest a shot of whiskey, but the laudanum would probably work better.

Crofton's voice was already slower and more drowsy from the drug as he said, "Fury . . ."

"Right here."

"I got to be sure about something . . . You said your name was . . . John Fury."

"That's right."

"The same John Fury who . . . rode with Fremont and Kit Carson?"

"I know them," Fury said simply.

"And had a run-in with Cougar Johnson in Santa Fe?"

"Yes."

"Traded slugs with Hemp Collier in San Antone last year?"

"He started the fight, didn't give me much choice but to finish it."

"Thought so." Crofton's hand lifted and clutched weakly at Fury's sleeve. "You got to . . . make me a promise."

Fury didn't like the sound of that. Promises made to dying men usually led to a hell of a lot of trouble.

Crofton went on, "You got to give me . . . your word . . . that you'll take these folks through . . . to where they're goin'."

"I'm no wagonmaster," Fury said.

"You know the frontier," Crofton insisted. Anger gave him strength, made him rally enough to lift his head from the ground and glare at Fury. "You can get 'em through. I know you can."

"Don't excite him," warned the gray-haired doctor.

"Why the hell not?" Fury snapped, glancing up at the physician. He noticed now that the man had his arm around the shoulders of a pretty red-headed girl in her teens, probably his daughter. He went on, "What harm's it going to do?"

The girl exclaimed, "Oh! How can you be so . . . so callous?"

Crofton said, "Fury's just bein' practical, Carrie. He knows we got to . . . got to hash this out now. Only chance

180

we'll get." He looked at Fury again. "I can't make you promise, but it . . . it'd sure set my mind at ease while I'm passin' over if I knew you'd take care of these folks."

Fury sighed. It was rare for him to promise anything to anybody. Giving your word was a quick way of getting in over your head in somebody else's problems. But Crofton was dying, and even though they had never crossed paths before, Fury recognized in the old man a fellow Westerner.

"All right," he said.

A little shudder ran through Crofton's battered body, and he rested his head back against the grassy ground. "Thanks," he said, the word gusting out of him along with a ragged breath.

"Where are you headed?" Fury figured the immigrants could tell him, but he wanted to hear the destination from Crofton.

"Colorado Territory . . . Folks figure to start 'em a town . . . somewhere on the South Platte. Won't be hard for you to find . . . a good place."

No, it wouldn't, Fury thought. No wagon train journey could be called easy, but at least this one wouldn't have to deal with crossing mountains, just prairie.

Prairie filled with savages and outlaws, that is.

A grim smile plucked at Fury's mouth as that thought crossed his mind. "Anything else you need to tell me?" he asked Crofton.

The wagonmaster shook his head and let his eyelids slide closed. "Nope. Figger I'll rest a spell now. We can talk again later."

"Sure," Fury said softly, knowing that in all likelihood, Leander Crofton would never wake up from this rest.

Less than a minute later, Crofton coughed suddenly, a wracking sound. His head twisted to the side, and blood welled for a few seconds from the corner of his mouth. Fury heard some of the women in the crowd cry out and turn away, and he suspected some of the men did, too.

"Well, that's all," he said, straightening easily from his kneeling position beside Crofton's body. He looked at the doctor. The red-headed teenager had her face pressed to the front of her father's shirt and her shoulders were shaking with sobs. She wasn't the only one crying, and even the ones who were dry-eyed still looked plenty grim.

"We'll have a funeral service as soon as a grave is dug," said the doctor. "Then I suppose we'll be moving on. You should know, Mr. . . . Fury was it? You should know that none of us will hold you to that promise you made to Mr. Crofton."

Fury shrugged. "Didn't ask if you intended to or not. I'm the one who made the promise. Reckon I'll keep it."

He saw surprise on some of the faces watching him. All of these travelers had probably figured him for some sort of drifter. Well, that was fair enough. Drifting was what he did best.

But that didn't mean he was a man who ignored promises. He had given his word, and there was no way he could back out now.

He met the startled stare of the doctor and went on, "Who's the captain here? You?"

"No, I . . . You see, we hadn't gotten around to electing a captain yet. We only left Independence a couple of weeks ago, and we were all happy with the leadership of Mr. Crofton. We didn't see the need to select a captain."

Crofton should have insisted on it, Fury thought with a grimace. You never could tell when trouble would pop up. Crofton's body lying on the ground was grisly proof of that.

Fury looked around at the crowd. From the number of people standing there, he figured most of the wagons in the train were at least represented in this gathering. Lifting his voice, he said, "You all heard what Crofton asked me to do. I gave him my word I'd take over this wagon train and get it on through to Colorado Territory. Anybody got any objection to that?"

His gaze moved over the faces of the men and women who were standing and looking silently back at him. The silence was awkward and heavy. No one was objecting, but Fury could tell they weren't too happy with this unexpected turn of events.

Well, he thought, when he had rolled out of his soogans that morning, he hadn't expected to be in charge of a wagon

182

train full of strangers before the day was over.

The gray-haired doctor was the first one to find his voice. "We can't speak for everyone on the train, Mr. Fury," he said. "But I don't know you, sir, and I have some reservations about turning over the welfare of my daughter and myself to a total stranger."

Several others in the crowd nodded in agreement with the sentiment expressed by the physician.

"Crofton knew me."

"He knew you have a reputation as some sort of gunman!"

Fury took a deep breath and wished to hell he had come along after Crofton was already dead. Then he wouldn't be saddled with a pledge to take care of these people.

"I'm not wanted by the law," he said. "That's more than a lot of men out here on the frontier can say, especially those who have been here for as long as I have. Like I said, I'm not looking to cause trouble. I was riding along and minding my own business when I came across you people. There's too many of you for me to fight. You want to start out toward Colorado on your own, I can't stop you. But you're going to have to learn a hell of a lot in a hurry."

"What do you mean by that?"

Fury smiled grimly. "For one thing, if you stop spread out like this, you're making a target of yourselves for every Indian in these parts who wants a few fresh scalps for his lodge." He looked pointedly at the long red hair of the doctor's daughter. Carrie—that was what Crofton had called her, Fury remembered.

Her father paled a little, and another man said, "I didn't think there was any Indians this far east." Other murmurs of concern came from the crowd.

Fury knew he had gotten through to them. But before any of them had a chance to say that he should honor his promise to Crofton and take over, the sound of hoofbeats made him turn quickly.

A man was riding hard toward the wagon train from the west, leaning over the neck of his horse and urging it on to greater speed. The brim of his hat was blown back by the wind of his passage, and Fury saw anxious, dark brown features underneath it. The newcomer galloped up to the crowd gathered next to the lead wagon, hauled his lathered mount to a halt, and dropped lithely from the saddle. His eyes went wide with shock when he saw Crofton's body on the ground, and then his gaze flicked to Fury.

"You son of a bitch!" he howled.

And his hand darted toward the gun holstered on his hip.